A Regency Novella

by

Shannon Donnelly

Copyright © 2019 by Shannon Donnelly. All rights reserved. This book or any portion thereof may not be reproduced or used in any manner whatsoever without the express written permission of the publisher except for the use of brief quotations in a book review.
Printed in the United States of America

First Printing, 2019
print ISBN: 9781077608863
Cielito Lindo Press

Cover by What the Hay Designs—whatthehay.com

A too-perfect duke, a very imperfect lady…is it the perfect match or a perfect disaster?

A duke in need of a wife…
The dukes of Everley always marry at thirty--but the current duke has left choosing a bride far too late. Arriving at a country house party for a Valentine's ball, he expects to find one suitable young lady to be the next duchess. He doesn't expect to find the woman he once kissed in a garden—the woman who was the bane of his life for a season and who might be the only woman who can save him from becoming a far too proper duke.

A lady in need of her own life…
Davinia has never forgotten that one kiss in a garden—but she has also been married and widowed and intends to keep her niece from making the mistake she nearly made when she allowed the Duke of Everley to kiss her. But when the house becomes snow-bound, Davinia begins to realize there is a warm-hearted man under the weight of a title. Is it too late to correct past mistakes and rekindle a love she thought lost?

To my own Valentine—Sammy.

*"Love is not love
Which alters it when alteration finds,
Or bends with the remover to remove:
O no! it is an ever-fixed mark
That looks on tempests and is never shaken..."*
— Shakespeare

Chapter One

I need a wife—and damnably soon.

The thought chased through Everley's head and had him tightening his fingers into a fist, but he only kept staring at the invitations on his desk.

Ian Morley Valentine Philip Wycliffe, Duke of Everley, Marquis of Levisham, Earl Colburn, and Baron Sutton—there was no viscountcy in the family for his ancestors had thought it a shoddy minor title—started to drum his fingers and stopped. Invitations had been sorted into neat stacks, and the clock in the hall chimed ten of the morning, which on the first and third Tuesday of the month meant his schedule called for a review of the demands upon his time for the following fortnight. Dudley Fanshaw—his secretary—was droning on about upcoming responsibilities. Everley could not attend him. One particular invitation—scented maddeningly enough with roses—was nagging like a bad tooth. He kept staring at the fine handwriting in a slanting, bold black.

The Countess of Somerton requests the pleasure of your attendance at a Valentine's Day ball and house party at Somerton.

Somerton? That name stirred a memory with uneasy associations. He looked up and asked his secretary. "Why is the Somerton invitation in my will-attend pile?"

Dudley blinked. Twice. A frisson of impatience caught at Everley, but he knew better than to express it. One did not treat those in one's employ with anything but firm courtesy. He could almost hear his father saying those words. Still, Dudley cleared his throat as if nervous and straightened his spectacles.

He was the younger son of a marquis who had been a crony of Everley's father. How exactly Dudley had come into Everley's employ, Everley could not quite say. They had not been together at Eton—Dudley was only twenty, while Everley had already celebrated his thirtieth year upon this earth. But a duke must have a secretary, and somehow Dudley's name had come up at the right time—the duke's former secretary had left to get himself married.

Everley wanted to sigh but didn't.

Thirty, he knew, was the age to marry. His father had told him so, his grandfather had been married at that age, and his great-grandfather, too. There might have been a generation that had skipped the habit, but Everley was hard put to recall any particular name. Wycliffe men married at thirty—a sensible age to get a wife and set up a nursery. He'd turned thirty just last September, hence his consideration of any invitation that made it to his desk. He had to find himself a wife, and he was running short of time if he was to meet the tradition set upon his shoulders by his forefathers.

Why, with all the marriage-minded mothers thrusting daughters into his path, had he left this so damnably late? Ah, but that was the answer as well as the question. All those marriage-minded mothers had left him adept at sidestepping possible entrapments. He'd had the notion he would find a wife in his own time, but he'd left it so late that time was now in rather short supply.

He tapped the Somerton invitation card on its edge.

Everley counted upon his secretary to handle the more mundane correspondence, to weed out invitations that presented unnecessary obligation—or such boring company as to make a vicar ready to snooze—and to smooth minor details. The fact that this invitation had made it past Dudley's screening meant it presented a greater demand upon the duke's attention than a dozen others that had been politely declined.

After clearing his throat again, Dudley said, "Somerton's estate marches with your holdings in Yorkshire. The North Riding."

Everley frowned. The end of nowhere. He recalled the land. A small property, only a few hundred acres with a charming manor house that dated to the sixteen hundreds—and therefore not completely without comforts—and a set of tenant farmers with rather a lot of sheep. He also could remember some disastrous ball he had once held for the locals. His forehead tightened. Some hoyden had—

Ah, yes, now he had it...Davinia. Of course it would have been Davinia. Her father had just come into the title back then, and was not the family name Edgerton?

He rubbed at the tightness on his brow, and his heart beat a little faster.

The Divine Davinia, she'd been called when she had made her bow to society. Tall as an Amazon, graceful—well, no she hadn't been that, but she had been rather like a comet, brilliant and searing hot across the social scene. Her laugh had turned heads. Her smile had seemed to warm a room. She had also been about as destructive as a comet when it went from shooting across the sky to hitting the ground as a meteor. She had been the bane of his life for a season, always seeming to be there, laughing, tormenting, being...well, being Davinia.

She had made a wreck of his life, his peace, his... But then she had vanished.

He'd heard she had gotten herself married to some nobody—a military or navy man or something like. He had done his best to forget her. She had...upset his world. His father had still been alive at the time, but had been ill with the dropsy that had eventually ended his days, and Everley had had his hands full, what with taking on the management of the vast estates that came with the dukedom and the other titles. That had helped him get through that dreadful year and the next and the next after that.

However, he had never truly forgotten Davinia, or their last and almost ruinous meeting in a garden. If there was a possibility she might be at Somerton, her brother's estate...? His stomach clenched, and a shiver slipped down his spine. Despite his need to find a bride, he put the invitation into the start of a will-not-attend pile. Davinia was not someone he would welcome back into his sphere. She really ought to have been called the Disastrous Davinia.

Dudley was now clearing his throat with meaningful insistence. "Beg pardon, your grace, but as you will recall, the Earl of Somerton has a daughter and no sons. The lands are also unentitled."

Everley frowned. He smoothed the expression at once. Dukes must be above showing such crude emotions as displeasure—or pleasure. He could just about hear his father saying that as well. Of course, a duke might give vent to some strong feeling but only if alone, and Everley had Dudley's presence to consider.

"Meaning...?" He lifted one eyebrow and let the

word trail off. Dudley would get around to things in time. He always did.

Dudley got around to it faster than usual. "There is a connection to trade, through the current earl's late mother, but the family has since abandoned all such undesirable ties, and I believe Somerton's daughter is on your short list. Lady Susan is also close friends with the two other candidates."

Everley's stare drifted to his desk—a dark mahogany, a practical and fine piece of workmanship as befit a duke. Wycliffe men had no need to stoop to ostentation. The room matched the desk in functionality—bookcases and a fine Adams fireplace—and restrained taste with walls of white plaster and only one thick carpet. On the desk, in another stack of unfinished business, lay the list that Everley had started two years ago. Damn, but he ought to have started it a half-dozen years ago. However, he'd put it off—and off again. Davinia really had soured him on…ah, but he should not blame her for his indolence. Now the list haunted him.

Four dozen names of possible duchesses.

He'd crossed off most names already—too old, too young, too close a connection and too far. Just last autumn, he'd finally arrived at the short list—four names of ladies of good breeding who might fit the role of a perfect duchess. Irritatingly enough, he'd had to strike through one name when Lady Amanda Croft had eloped with a banker's son. However, three names remained.

Pulling out the sheet of fine rag paper—embossed with his crest on the top and written in his own careful hand with a line of black ink across most of the names—he scanned the list. Yes, indeed, there was

Lady Susan, only child of the Earl of Somerton. The old duke would have issued a warning about her background what with that hint of trade, but these days it must be admitted that money had to be made from something other than land. Everley had faced that unpleasant fact already. Estates might be looked to for generating income as they always had before this modern era, but lands also required upkeep and investment to keep them profitable. One also could not forget one's obligations to churches and charities. That was where he greatly required a duchess to help manage such things for him, as well as to provide a suitable heir for the dukedom.

Besides, he would be thirty-one soon. It was time he married to maintain the tradition just as he must uphold all other Wycliffe traditions. His hand had fisted again, and he forced his fingers open and smoothed the paper he had almost crumpled. It was odd that he could not keep a single name on his short list in mind.

He glanced at Dudley.

The man came of good stock himself. He wore his brown hair short but so closely cropped that he might be taken for a sporting fellow. His wide-spaced blue eyes held some intelligence. He dressed neatly, as befit a secretary to the Duke of Everley—a blue coat for town, a brown for the country, tan breeches and plain, white silk stockings. A buff waistcoat—Everley disliked pretentions to dandyism—and black shoes. Boots when traveling. Everley did not hold with the new fashion for pantaloons—they looked…tight. Breeches had been good enough for the ten previous dukes. Well, one of them might have worn a codpiece, but that fellow had been the exception to almost everything in the family. He had also been the Wycliffe whose portrait had been banished to the attic, and no one mentioned him unless to hold him up as a bad example of pretty much everything.

Everley glanced at his list. "Do you expect the non-Somerton girls will be at this house party?"

Dudley nodded, seemed to recall that was not much of an answer, and said, his voice smooth and unhurried, "Highly likely, your grace. And one lady will no doubt meet or exceed your expectations."

Expectations! For a mad moment, Everley wanted to crumple up his list and toss it into the fire. Damnable expectations. Was he not bound utterly by them?

These momentary fits had been with him for as long as he could recall—the urge to kick over the traces, to do the unexpected. To throw everything to the wind. To dash expectations to the ground and just…well, he knew not what, for he had never done any such thing. Or almost never. This had to be the inheritance of that Elizabethan ancestor—the one who had sported a codpiece and had been a dashed loose screw by all accounts—cropping up. Nothing more. Even thinned as it was by proper alliances, that man's blood still ran in Everley's veins and had to be mastered. His father, the late duke, had urged Everley with words—and sometimes a strip of birch—to curb such impulses.

Life is about nothing more than meeting all expectations.

God, he hated that phrase. But it was the truth. Everley pulled in a breath—or tried to, for it caught in his throat. He pressed his palm flat on the cool, firm wood of his desk. It did not help.

Standing, he left the invitations and his list where they lay. He put a hand over the papers. For an instant, he glimpsed his father's signet ring on his hand—the seal of carved onyx, black as the Devil's eye—and it seemed to be on his father's index finger. Long, narrow backed hands, slim wrists, and that damn ring—the burden of a dukedom.

He had relatives petitioning him for favors, royals to attend, estates needing repairs that emptied his coffers almost as fast as they filled them, and duties…endless duties. He was head of his family, responsible for finding careers and postings for younger sons, smoothing the path of those in the family with political ambitions, and approving alliances for daughters and nieces and those with even slimmer blood ties. He was always supposed to set an example of virtue, industry, and just the right amount of aid to the poor that he might face the vicars who served in his parishes without guilt, but not so much that he would be deemed a 'soft touch' by the world in general.

Today, he couldn't bear it another second.

Chest tight, heart thudding, unable to breathe, he strode for the door, brushing past poor Dudley, who shook his head and let out a sigh. Dudley had seen this before, and Everley's face burned because of that.

He called for his curricle to be brought around to the front at once and paced the hall as footmen and porters hurried to the mews behind his London house—the duke's London residence was both vast and unfashionably to the north of town, where there was land enough for gardens and stables—to see his orders obeyed. Everley needed the rush of wind past his face. He needed pounding hooves obliterating his thoughts. He needed the sense that, even if the rest of his life was tightly proscribed, he could at least find some measure of liberty with his horses.

Dudley's voice called him back to his duty. "Your grace, how shall I answer Somerton? The invitation is neither in the acceptance nor the rejection stack."

Everley glanced at Dudley, standing patiently in the doorway to the study, hands folded behind his back and the light from the windows glinting off his spectacles. Looking past the man, Everley saw his desk. A small shock went through him, like the jolt of a punch landing hard against his solar plexus. He never left anything disordered—never. But this time he had.

Skin chilled and mouth dry, he could only think, *I must get out.*

He waved a hand. "I must marry before the end of summer if I am to marry at thirty, and I'm certain one of them will make a perfect duchess. I'll attend."

Bolting for the out-of-doors, he hoped for at least a taste of cool air. However, he knew whatever path he took would only lead him back here to responsibilities and the nagging horror that someday he would fail his father's memory and that of every Wycliffe before him. Every one except that dashed loose screw.

Chapter Two

Davinia had escaped the duke's arrival—or so she hoped. At least for now, she had her freedom. She slapped the reins on the rump of the dappled-grey pony, Gertie, who picked up her pace to a brisk trot. Crisp and chill, a breeze stung her cheeks, but a blue sky dazzled overhead. After two days of rain and ice, Davinia simply could not stand waiting at the house another moment. Guests would be arriving today...including the Duke of Everley. She wrinkled her nose and told herself not to be so judgmental when it came to that man. Perhaps he had changed. Perhaps he had *not* grown into a perfectly stiff and stuffy copy of his father. Yes, and perhaps Gertie would grow wings today as well to fly over these muddy roads. Would that not also be fabulously wonderful?

A fox darted across the track that wound its way to Mersey, the nearest village, twelve miles down the lane from Somerton. Gertie snorted an objection to the flash of red, and Davinia put her focus on keeping the mare firm in the traces. The shooting cart was really Freddy's, but Freddy's idea of shooting was to escape the house with dogs at his heels, gaiters on, and to come back covered in dirt, grinning, hounds exhausted and panting, and not so much as a feather in his game bag. Which meant poor Gertie—a cob perfect for the cart but a touch small to ride—never got out enough. Davinia was quite happy to provide Gertie with exercise and herself the distraction of going to Mersey for the ribbons Felicity wanted and had forgotten.

"Pink and red and white," her sister-in-law had

ordered. "Or do you think that too much?"

Davinia did think it a bit much, what with Felicity nursing pink and white and red roses into early bloom in the hothouse and now set on having the servants dot Somerton with the fragrant results. With Felicity's plans, Valentine's Day promised to be rather cloyingly sentimental. However, the Countess of Somerton must have her wishes granted, and so Davinia had merely smiled and said she would do her best. She adored Felicity, but might she convince her sister-in-law that only gold or silver ribbon could be had in Mersey? Or perhaps that there was not the need to make every room in Somerton into an overly fragrant bower dedicated to love?

Davinia gave a snort. She doubted any of that, but the trip to Mersey at least promised momentary relief.

It was a small enough village what with one dressmaker, one church—Anglican, of course—a shop that tried to offer bits of everything and not much of anything, an inn that also provided a blacksmith's skills, a confectioner's that served up delectable baked goods, and three pubs that filled to capacity on market day. The excuse of lack might serve. Davinia was considering if Felicity could be convinced of such a tale when the neigh of a horse and the splash of hooves in mud had her slowing Gertie with a gentling voice.

The lane—narrow and bound by hedges planted thirty years ago when a good part of this land had been enclosed—curved with an S-like bend. Gertie's ears pricked forward with a show of interest, and Davinia slowed the mare to a walk. Around the next curve, the cause of the commotion came into view.

A carriage had overturned. Not just a carriage but

a traveling chaise. Davinia could just glimpse the crest on a black lacquer door now pointing skyward. Her pulse quickened. Carriage accidents could be horrid things. She had seen one once, an overturned phaeton that had left one young man with a broken arm and a lady screaming in hysterics. Davinia's stomach tightened, but now was not a time to be sick over such thoughts.

She transferred her stare to the horses.

A team of four bays with flashy white socks fretted in the road, their harness not yet tangled. The panic bubbling inside Davinia settled into a knot of anger and disgust. Old Tom was up to his tricks again—and that near leader, holding up his leg as if he'd lamed himself, was as fine an actor as his master back at the posting inn on the edge of Mersey.

Drawing Gertie to a halt, Davinia parted her lips to offer assistance such as she might give, but a gentleman shifted his stance in the lane, moving from the shadowing trees into pale sunlight, and she forgot everything else but that tall, straight figure. Her heart gave a sharp jolt, and her mouth dried. She would know that rather handsome back—with the broad shoulders, tapering waist, and superb tailoring—anywhere.

His Grace the Duke of Everley, Marquis of Levisham, Earl Colburn, and Baron whatever else he was, stood with his hat in his hand, thumping it against his thigh. The impressive cut of his coat, the gleam of his boots, and his straight, black hair seemed perfect as ever. He stood three-quarters profile to her, and she knew the width of his shoulders owed nothing to padding and everything to the muscle he had honed. She'd once had her hands on those broad shoulders, and oh, but that thought should not make her breath catch as if she was still a green girl. She tried to focus on other memories—such as the condemnation her mother had always shown for idle lords—but those shoulders of his kept distracting. Boxing and fencing were the sports of gentlemen, and the dukes of Everley, as she knew from every gossip rag in England, always presented an image to the world of the ideal manly figure. It was a shame that perfection gave them no sympathy for anyone else's flaws.

A flush of heat shot up Davinia's neck along with sudden and stinging awareness of her own imperfections. Why did she feel a girl of eighteen, mortified at meeting a duke, and being pushed forward into society simply because her father had come into the title unexpectedly? Every embarrassment from her first ball to her last, every gauche moment of the wrong curtsy or address, every accident she'd blundered into kept swimming from memory.

Lud, but she'd been a calamity.

However, she was a widow now—Charles, bless him, had been gone these past two years, killed while he served on the HMS *Monarch* during a battle near the Bay of Biscay. That tragic news had struck Davinia hard but had hit her mother even harder, for she'd doted on Charles. Davinia had been left to nurse her mother through her final sickness—her father had passed on two years prior. She had come to live with her brother and sister-in-law only recently so she might help launch her niece. However, she was no longer the girl who'd escaped that dreadful scrape with Everley, and the even worse scene with his family.

Gertie tossed her head, jingling the harness, and Davinia forced her gloved fingers to relax. The rattling pulled Everley's stare from his mishap and to Davinia's cart. His frown deepened, and he lifted his chin a fraction.

For a mad second, those dark eyes of his fixed on her. Davinia wanted to jump down from the cart, drag Gertie's head around, and bolt back to Somerton. The narrow lane made that utterly impossible. There was sufficient room to turn a mount but not a horse and cart. Besides, Somerton offered no escape, for that must be Everley's destination. Forcing her spine straight, Davinia told herself she must not run from him. She had done so once—in tears and distraught. Well, twice actually from his person and once from his letters. Never again.

Managing to find a smile, she called out, "May I be of assistance?"

Still frowning—oh, did the man even own a smile?—Everley strode to the shooting cart. His perfection had been marred, and Davinia's mouth twitched to see it. Mud streaked his buff breeches and caked one side of his right boot. His hat looked crumpled—no wonder he carried it instead of wearing it. He'd dressed for travel in a greatcoat that hung open to show a black coat underneath and a plain yellow waistcoat—all immaculate, the quality boasted only by the fine material and close fit. His cravat, however, looked much tugged upon and his hair—oh, drat, but his hair was being swept by the breeze into the most romantic disorder. If Susan ever saw him this way, she'd swoon over that straight, commanding nose and that firm jaw line and that dratted handsome face with those wide, dark eyes. Davinia had once had the same reaction. She took a breath to steady herself.

Everley stopped beside the cart and had to look up slightly to meet Davinia's stare. "Davinia." His mouth curved ever so slightly after he spoke her name, as if it did so without him wanting it to.

She flushed hot, then cold. Swallowing hard, she cleared her throat. "It is Mrs. Charles Davenport now." She would have that much respect from him.

He swept a small, oh-so-correct bow. "I beg your pardon. I had heard you had married but not the particulars."

"Of course you wouldn't care, would you?" She bit down on her lower lip and shook her head. She should not start swiping at him without cause. Time to put away the claws. "But let's not drag out ancient history. You changed horses at the Brown Boar in Mersey, did you not? Someone ought to have warned you of Old Tom's tricks."

Everley had glanced back at his traveling coach, on its side in the mud, but now he looked at Davinia, one dark eyebrow lifted. His eyes were even blacker than she remembered—dark as jet, she thought. He had the Everley aristocratic nose, an uncompromising chin just like his father's that jutted forward ever so slightly, and only the fullness of his lower lip softened his features. His lips flattened for a moment—with disapproval, she thought—and he asked, "Old Tom?"

"The innkeeper and a devil if he sees money to be had." She gave a nod to the team of bays. "They're notorious in these parts. But if Old Tom sees a gentleman from London, he'll do what he must to harness these four to the carriage. The near leader—that fellow holding up his leg as if he's broken it—will limp all the way home, but he'll trot sound as soon as Old Tom has him back in his care and taps just the right spot on his shoulder. The wheelers also both know to shy at sharp curves, slacking in their traces and then bolting ahead, which is how you ended in a ditch. Old Tom will demand payment for the lame horses and even more for the repairs to your coach. He's soaked more than one gentleman with this trick."

Everley's jaw had tightened and the pulse began to pound at the spot where his cheek met his ear. His eyes narrowed, and now Davinia wondered if she ought to have mentioned anything about Old Tom's tricks. Perhaps she should have left well enough alone. She had remembered Everley's arrogance—and that of his high-in-the-instep father—but she had not recalled Everley had ever been a bad man to cross. Just now, however, he looked downright dangerous.

Shifting on the cart's padded bench and settling the reins in one hand, she patted the seat beside her with her other gloved hand. "Come, Everley. Looking daggers at those poor post boys will not right the situation. They are paid by Old Tom and would lose their jobs if they did not follow orders. The lane is narrow, but so is the cart. I think we may slip past. There's a turning ahead that will lead us back around and put us on our way to Somerton, and Freddy…that is, my brother will send someone to right and fetch your coach. We may send the horses and post boys back to the Brown Boar, and Freddy's grooms will bring your team from the inn to our stables if that is what you wish. What say you?"

Everley turned to face her, his black eyes so dark she could barely make out where the iris began and the pupils ended. He shook his head. "That will most certainly not do." He started back to the wrecked carriage, his stride long, and Davinia let out a sigh.

He hadn't changed a bit. He was still that overbearing, pompous, righteous idiot she had bolted from in the garden of his house after that disastrous argument between her mother and the old duke, and he was about to make a mull of this.

How in all creation could Felicity ever be considering him as a possible husband for Susan? That most certainly would be a mistake. But could either event—Everley's anger now or Susan's potential and expected infatuation with a duke—be stopped?

Chapter Three

Mud squishing under his boots, Everley halted in front of the lame team—or the pretending lame horse and the pretending shying ones—and his overturned carriage. He did not think of himself as a hard man. *One is obligated by position to use firm courtesy at all times.* Another of his father's homilies. He could also feel Davinia's stare upon his back.

Why in blazes did she think she had a right to judge him?

A frisson of impatience caught at Everley, sizzling under his skin like the brush of thistles. It perhaps fixed his mouth into a harsher line than he intended.

The horses stopped fussing and eyed him. The post boys—one on foot just now and one still mounted—stopped squabbling about the fault for the accident and swapped uneasy glances. Everley sent up a wish that he might keep his own horses on every damnable cross-roads in the country, but that would be an absurd expense. The dukes of Everley had not acquired position with a foolish squandering of resources. However, these…these villains might have killed him with this accident.

He deepened his frown. Faces paled. When he was certain he had everyone's full attention, he gave a nod. "Shall we sort matters? How much does this…Old Tom pay you?"

The post boys traded glances. The one holding the near leader turned to Everley shook his head and said with just a shade too much raw innocence in his voice, "Pay, my lord? You meanin' as post boys?"

"You may address me as your grace, lad, and I mean for this nasty turn. Now do I summon the local constables, the magistrate, the lord lieutenant and whomever else I must, or will you answer?"

The lad—a blackamoor with a gap between his front teeth—swallowed hard and pulled off his cap with one hand. He was wise enough to keep his other hand on the reins of the horse he was holding. He glanced over at the shooting cart that now stood behind Everley and said, "Davinia peached on us, did she?"

"You will leave Mrs. Davenport out of this. Do you know the penalties for fraud?"

The boys glanced at each other yet again. Neither of them looked to be past the age of twenty—young enough to be scared and thin enough to need every meal they could come by. Everley tapped his hat against his thigh. He wanted to pull at his cravat, or turn toward Davinia—Mrs. Davenport—and tell her to please stop staring at him.

Why, after what must be almost five years apart, did he still know she would be wishing for him to let these young scoundrels off lightly? That simply would not do. He had a duty. *Wrong doing must never be tolerated.* Somehow, Davinia's stare was overriding the ghostly echo of his father's grave tones.

Pushing out a breath, he told the lads, "I could have you transported for life. And if I had come to harm in that accident—murder is a hanging offense, lads. If you had killed a duke—"

"It were an accident, my...yer grace," the other lad, fair as the other boy was dark, blurted out. He sat mounted on one of the wheelers, looking as if he had been born in a saddle.

Everley turned a stare on him, and the lad slumped low. He was even thinner and smaller than his compatriot in crime. Mouth pressed tight, Everley fought the desire to let this incident pass as Davinia might wish. Instead, he said, "You will unharness this team and use whatever trick you use to make them sound again. Take them back to Old Tom with a warning that if I ever hear of so much as a wheel that's nicked a tree from any carriage he has harnessed, I will see the full weight of the law falls not just on him but on everyone in his employ. I will see him in prison and his worldly goods taken from him to provide restitution to anyone hurt in such an accident be it genuine or arranged."

The blackamoor lad chewed on his lower lip. "My lo...I means, yer gracefulness, what's resty-too-shun?" He stumbled over the word.

Everley raised one eyebrow and resisted lifting his eyes to heaven in a silent prayer for forbearance. Such a gesture was not fitting for a duke, but even a duke might have his limits. "It is fair payment to address a wrong and a term you need to add to your vocabulary. Now off with you. Fetch my horses and lead them to Somerton. I should not have changed the team in Mersey, but they were looking tired and had come a good distance from the main road north. See they arrive safely, and I shall call this a lesson for us all. And may you take this as a sign you need to find an honest master."

Nodding, the darker lad slapped on his cap and had the team unhitched faster than Everley would have thought possible. The post boy swung back up into his postilion's saddle and turned the team for Mersey. At a touch on his right shoulder near the withers, the lame leader stopped limping and grunting, the other three horses at once settled into order and they trotted off as if well schooled. Which they must be, Everley realized, to pull off such a vile trap as this.

Turning, he strode back to Davinia—to Mrs. Davenport. And why could he not remember she had wed another? He ought to. She wore grey as suited a widow. A lovely shade that matched her eyes. He glanced up at her, expecting that look of hers—the disappointed frown that had haunted him the year he'd known her in London. Instead, she tipped her head to one side and seemed to regard him with a touch of amusement...and was that actual respect?

"That was well done of you," she said. "Although you sounded rather stiff necked—'you may address me as your grace' indeed."

As always, the sound of her voice tugged on him and left him wanting to smile. She had a low, throaty voice, not one of those shrill tones that grated on a man's nerves. He put a hand on the dash of the shooting cart. "Meaning you did not expect any forgiveness from me? I do have a few Christian values to my soul."

"Well...no, I did not expect...but it is not a bad thing to exceed expectations. Is that not always your goal?"

He gave her a brief, polite smile—a small upturn of the lips—and hauled himself into the cart. He put his hat on the seat between them—not as good as a shield against her charms but better than nothing—and held out his hand. "I shall be happy to take the reins from you and exceed even more so by getting us around my poor traveling chaise, which is half off the road and has made quite a dent in that hedge. It will take a few strong men to pull it upright again."

She did not relinquish the reins. "It is a good thing you travel alone. You have no luggage with you? No servants?"

He frowned. "What? I must travel with my entire household, outriders, and a full equipage as befits my station?" In truth, he'd sent word ahead to ready the house on his estate nearby should he have need of it to extend his stay—or to escape this house party. His valet and personal items were due to arrive at Somerton later in the day, but he saw no reason why he should inform Davinia of such a thing. She'd no doubt only think him top-lofty for simply having more than one household to his name.

Head tipped still to one side, bonnet ribbons fluttering in the breeze, Davinia kept a steady regard on him. He almost wanted to squirm in his seat. "Actually, I was thinking more of the stories of bones broken, not from a carriage tipping over but from the clash of one body upon another. I also think Gertie knows my hand better than yours." She threaded the leather reins through her gloves—also in a soft, dove gray—and Gertie tossed her head as if agreeing, or wishing to be on her way.

With a shake of his head, he said, "You will have us tangled in the hedge opposite my coach if you insist on this. You know you will. Come now, you must admit I am the better whip. You may point the way, and I shall drive us to Somerton." He put his hand over hers.

That was a mistake.

The sun might be struggling for warmth but not so her hand. He could feel the heat of her body, and a tremor slipped through her fingers. Surely she was not frightened of him. He watched her closely. Her cheeks brightened with a wash of pink that left her looking more the girl she had been. Her stare flew up to meet his, her eyes wide and her lips parted. His pulse skipped to a faster beat. For an instant, it seemed he was again sitting with her on that damnable bench in that damnable garden behind that damnable townhouse in London, her scent of lavender weaving around him, intoxicating and entrancing.

That ancient spark of something between them flared—the unseemly attraction that had pulled him to her like the call of a siren luring a sailor to his doom on the rocks. He could not explain it. Perhaps that adage that came from some scientific fellow about opposites attracting held some truth. Perhaps this allure could be ascribed to nothing more than a physical reaction. Perhaps the legacy of that dashed loose screw of an ancestor—the one held up to every generation in his family as a bad example—was simply resurfacing in his blood like an illness that could not be fully cured. Whatever this was, it had led to one indiscretion with Davinia, to less than perfect behavior, and to an intolerable embarrassment for them both that had almost wrecked their lives. He hoped he was now both older and far wiser.

He pulled his hand away.

Davinia's cheeks turned an even brighter red. She wet her lips and let out a breath, and Everley braced himself for her words. Her mother had been quite the shrew and low-bred enough to give vent to every emotion that had ever flitted through her mind or heart. However, Davinia now proved herself more the lady. She merely turned her face to give him her profile, pressed her lips tight, and Everley was reminded that, for all her faults, Davinia was also an earl's daughter and sister to the current Earl of Somerton.

He faced forward and pressed his hands against his thighs, where they could damn well stay, and said, "Well, if you must drive, you must. How long do you think it will take us to reach Somerton?" He hoped the question—innocuous as it was—would set them back on safe ground. He glanced at Davinia. She was keeping her stare straight ahead as if fascinated by how the breeze flipped the cob's mane to one side and then another. However, he could see the pulse beating in her throat under the loose ribbons of her bonnet.

Instead of answering—or easing the cart past his overturned carriage—she slapped the reins upon the rump of the gray cob, clucked to the horse, and set the mare into a fast trot. He resisted the urge to clutch at the side railing of the cart. He also wanted to shut his eyes. An overturn twice in one day was almost more bad luck than he could bear.

But Davinia skirted past his carriage—bumping her wheels into a rut on the opposite side and scraping his shoulder against a low-hanging tree branch. He heard cloth tear and clenched his jaw against a curse. Blast it, but he had liked this particular greatcoat, and he could now feel the wind slipping through that tear, under one of the capes. He glanced at his left arm—a rip in the cloth itself and not a seam, so impossible to mend without it showing—and then he looked at Davinia.

She tipped up her chin, a satisfied smile on her lips. His heart gave a hard bump that could not be accounted for by the sway of the shooting cart. They bowled along, well past his carriage, the cob trotting smartly, flaxen mane flapping with each step. Everley started to say something cutting about how Davinia had not outgrown her habit of leaping into ill-advised risks, but he thought better of it. If he started down that path, there was no telling where it might end. He must remember he owed her his thanks for this rescue.

Leaning against the backrest of the cart bench, he started to talk about the weather and if she thought it must rain again soon, and would the roads hold out against more moisture or would they become utter mires. If nothing else, he could fight this attraction to her with dull, civil conversation.

He would behave himself, even if she could not be trusted to do so. He would go on proving himself worthy of his family name and his father's legacy of a proper upbringing. He would find himself a decent duchess at this blasted house party just as he must, and he would be able to part ways with Davinia again, this time with a thankful prayer for making such an escape a second time in his life.

But why oh why did he keep thinking about how soft her lips had once been under his—and why did he keep wondering what was going through her head and under that absurd bonnet of hers with its curling feathers and flopping ribbons?

Chapter Four

The weather?

Really—he could do no better?

The topic occupied the drive to Somerton, and Davinia listened to Everley going on and on about cloud patterns, how excessively cold this past winter had proven, and predictions from old broken bones that foretold more snow to come. When the iron gates of Somerton loomed ahead of them, she almost let out a relieved breath.

But only almost.

Everley, devil take the man, had one of those attractive, rumbling sorts of voices that seemed like rough velvet—smooth but with an interesting texture that compelled attention. She could listen to him lecture about the dullest things, which was what she was doing just now. She forced her attention back to Gertie, who had picked up her pace, for she knew this drive led back to the stables. It wouldn't do to allow Gertie to bolt for home.

Framed by tall yew hedges, the iron gates of Somerton stood open—Freddy never closed the gates—and one curve of the graveled lane brought the main house into view. The sight elicited a smile at once, for Somerton's beauty—even with winter not yet done—could not be ignored. Freddy had had the main gardens landscaped, doing away with the stiff, formal gardens so lawns and scattered oaks now offered what seemed a perfectly natural setting for the white stone of the house.

Somerton had been built as a square, upright

manor, and stood stiff as a beaten meringue. Davinia had never cared overmuch for the interior of the house—too many drafty rooms with high ceilings that made them impossible to heat. Besides, she had not grown up here. Her early memories included a crowded London townhouse always filled with noise and guests, cozy nooks, and books stuffed onto every shelf. Her father had loved to entertain, even if her mother had never cared for it, and her father had known everyone from artists and actors to old school chums to men in trade and adventurous travelers. Father had never taken notice of anyone's background—he had only wanted to know interesting people. Oddly, she could recall few women ever came to call, but that must have been due to her mother, who preferred to sit in a corner and sew, or who had Freddy or Davinia read to her of an evening from what Mother had called "improving works" with excessively moralizing sermons that had made Father pull faces.

Those ponderous works had been almost as unexciting as Everley's conversation just now.

Davinia pulled to a halt in front of the manor. Gertie stomped a hoof on the brushed gravel—she usually went straight to the stables and would be impatient for her oats. Glancing at Everley, Davinia tipped her head to one side. The grooms had not yet noticed their arrival, but footmen were already coming out of the house—guests were expected, after all. "Have you really no better a topic for me than the weather? No questions for me about where I've kept myself these past few years? No interest in if I'd been captured by pirates or swept away by the fairy folk like poor Tam Lin in the ballad?"

He looked at her—that gaze unsettling and direct

as always, the eyes dark with an odd touch of loneliness in the depths. That look had always caught at her and had led her into thinking it must be a rather friendless state to be not just an only child but one brought up by a cold father in an even colder household. She must be imagining such things, however, for he said in that deep voice of his, his tone prosaic as if still discussing the weather, "If you had been set upon by pirates, I would no doubt have read of your exploits in the newspaper. As to fairy folk, every version I ever heard gave me to understand you would be with them a hundred years and a day, and it has not been so long."

She laughed. "And such personal questions are so vulgar. You forgot that part."

The corner of his mouth twitched, or so she thought. But then Mercer, Freddy's butler, came bustling out, full of bows and more "your graces" than even Everley could possibly want—Mercer was terribly impressed with having a duke under the roof and seemed determined to impress. Davinia happily left the duke to Mercer's care—Freddy's butler could look after this most high and noble guest—and drove 'round to the stables. She stayed longer than she ought, fussing after Gertie, slipping a handful of oats to Freddy's hunter, who was growing disgracefully fat and lazy in his old age. Finally, Old Seb, the head groom, ushered her out by waving his cap at her and urging her in his broad north country tones to take herself off to be mitherin' somewhere else, as if she was a bother. Old Seb could be counted upon not to stand on ceremony with anyone.

She came into the house through the back, near to the kitchen, using the mud room where Freddy kept his guns and his gaiters for shooting. The room was small and wood paneled and smelled of musty dogs, but it offered quick access to the servant's stairs and up to her room so she might change. And think.

In her room, with the door shut, she could throw off her bonnet and gloves and pull off the riding habit she had worn on the drive. She tugged on a morning dress in forest green that was both old and favorite for its soft wool and warmth. She ought to ring for a maid to help and to tidy her hair, but no doubt Felicity would have the house upside-down to cater to the duke.

The day was still raw, and the fire in her room had been cleaned and reset for later in the evening but had not yet been lit. Davinia pulled a paisley shawl over her shoulders and curled up on the window seat to watch the other guests arrive.

She ought to go and break the news to Felicity of the failed quest for ribbons, but Felicity would have her hands full with Everley. Oh, bother Everley. Why must he go and accept this invitation of all invitations?

Felicity had been over the moon to have a duke attending her Valentine's house party. Davinia was not so happy. A country house party in February with the sky raw still, winter clinging, and the roads uncertain seemed folly to her. But Felicity had been determined. She wanted her daughter, Susan, to have an early start into society. Hence, invitations had been sent to several unmarried and very eligible gentlemen, including the duke.

Which meant Everley must be here to seek a bride. Davinia could not think why else he would come. Oh, he had property nearby, but he had visited it only once before—lud, that had been another disaster. She also knew him to be unmarried, for every movement of the 'Duke of E' was featured regularly in the *Morning*

Chronicle along with other news of the fashionable. Mother had scorned such gossip, but Davinia and Freddy had always made a game of guessing names out of it. It was no game, however, if Everley really was here to find a bride.

Davinia chewed on a thumbnail and let her thoughts turn to her niece.

At seventeen, Susan was a delight. But she was impulsive still and uncertain of herself. Not unlike myself, Davinia thought. She'd been awkward in society. Davinia's father had come into the title late in life, but Susan had been born after Freddy had come into the title and had been raised a lady. But what did Susan need from a husband? Someone with a sense of humor to match her own? Someone closer to her own age certainly. And what of the burden of a title?

Davinia wrinkled her nose.

Were mothers not always seeking the best for their daughters, even if the motherly idea of best did not match the daughter's heart and mind. Davinia knew too much of such a thing. Hadn't her own mother gone on and on about finding a worthy husband, meaning a man who had a profession? She'd been in alt when Charles had come along. Felicity seemed quite the opposite and ready to have her head turned by an offer from a duke, and Freddy would do whatever Felicity asked, for he liked his peaceful home far too much to upset his wife. All that meant Susan might well be pushed into an engagement with Everley simply because he was a duke.

Lud, hadn't she almost been trapped?

Leaving off fretting her thumbnail, Davinia stood and went to her dressing table. The thick carpet muffled her steps, but the worn floorboards squeaked as she crossed. She opened her jewel box and pulled out the gold locket she'd not worn in years—not since Charles had proposed to her. Working the latch, she had it click open. She stared at the pressed bluebell, its color faded and its faint scent long gone. She touched a finger to the dry flower, a reminder of a memory from a long-ago spring. Ah, but she was being maudlin. With a huffed breath, she snapped the locket closed. But she kept the cool gold oval in her hand and thought back to what she knew of Everley.

She could simply provoke Everley into showing his pompous side. That would not be difficult. She had done that often enough during her one disastrous season. But would it be enough to put Felicity—and Susan—off the man? Practical jokes of any sort were also straight out of it. Freddy and Susan would laugh, but Felicity would feel her party ruined, and Davinia could not be so horrible to her sister-in-law. Perhaps she could simply monopolize the duke's company? But that would prove her as vulgar as he must think her. Her father might have come into an unexpected earldom after the early demise of two older brothers, but Davinia still felt at times the social taint of being the daughter of a merchant's daughter. Well, perhaps Everley would consider Freddy's girl to be just as tainted by trade.

That proved not to be the case at dinner.

Long before the dinner bell rang, Davinia had changed into something fitting a widow—a watered silk in slate gray with a cream and flower-patterned shawl. She left her locket in her jewel box and chose to wear her mother's pearls instead. Mother had hated the pearls, but Father had bought them for her when he'd inherited the title, saying every lady needed a set of respectable jewelry. Freddy had insisted they go to Davinia after Mother's death, and Felicity had admitted she did not care for pearls, so that settled the matter. Davinia intended them to eventually go to Susan, but Susan did not need the sheen of pearls to appear lovely beyond measure.

Susan had been seated between Everley and Freddy's other neighbor, Lord Leifmere, a young man more Susan's age, but a mere viscount and not a duke. Leifmere also appeared to be utterly tongue-tied, or perhaps overly in awe of Susan, for he seemed unable to do more than reply to her in monosyllables. Everley, of course, had changed into exacting evening wear of a black coat and breeches, a gleaming white shirt, cravat and waistcoat, and black patent shoes, all of which meant his luggage and valet must have arrived. He carried on a perfectly correct conversation.

No doubt discussing the cold weather again, Davinia thought, and then bit the inside of her cheek. She really should not be so uncharitable.

Seated between Mrs. Mosby—a stout matron who enjoyed her food and whose conversation seemed restricted to requests to pass along various dishes and asking for the recipes for her own cook—and Mr. Tobin—the vicar and a gentleman renowned for his shyness unless one hit upon his favorite topic of his garden—Davinia had time to study the company.

Felicity had at least invited two of Susan's dearest friends to the party. Miss Amberson came in company with her parents, a rather thin and nervous Mrs. Amberson and the somewhat gruff Mr. Amberson, who applied himself to his food. Miss Mosby sat next to her brother, a young gentleman with aspirations to dandyism, to judge by his florid waistcoat and high shirt points, and her mother. Both young ladies faded in comparison to Susan, with one young miss being somewhat horse-faced and the other afflicted with an unfortunate, high-pitched giggle. Davinia put the too-often heard Mosby giggle down to nerves, and in truth Miss Amberson would look better as she aged and acquired style that might render her dramatic. A plain white gown did nothing to show her to advantage. Susan, however, looked as ideal as any young lady could wish with her pale, silver-blonde curls held up by a blue ribbon that matched her eyes and her dress. A hint of a smile curved her lips as she listened to something Everley was saying.

  A jolt stabbed into Davinia. She looked away. Surely she could not be jealous of Susan having caught Everley's attention. She glanced back to see Susan turn to Lord Leifmere. Susan was trying to pull the young man into the conversation with a question about if he thought Squire Meln would take the hunt out this week or would the ground be too hard with ice. That at least seemed to require more than a yes or no answer.

  Davinia tried to tame her wandering thoughts and reorder them. What if Susan was indeed attracted to Everley? It would have to be a fleeting thing, for how could such a match ever be satisfactory for either of them? Everley would bore Susan—or Susan would shock the man down to the soles of his polished patent-leather pumps. But an attraction might lead to something deeper—love might change everyone's expectations. Which meant she needed to draw out Susan on the topic and discover the girl's initial feelings on this matter.

  As soon as Felicity indicated the ladies should rise and retire to the drawing room, leaving the men to their port, Davinia made her way to Susan's side and drew her away from her friends with the excuse of wishing Susan's opinion on Davinia's latest embroidery disaster. Susan eyed the pattern of flowers and leaves that were somehow starting to look more like a green giraffe and then gave Davinia a direct stare. "You did not really want me to say anything about what you already know is a monstrosity."

With a smile, Davinia plucked at the embroidery. The room smelled of wood smoke from the fire and beeswax from the candles, both of which helped to take the chill from the air. The gentlemen would join them, no doubt adding a faint whiff of tobacco and port. Davinia tugged her shawl up over her shoulder. "If you won't give me your thoughts on this, what about those on the gentlemen here tonight?"

"Is there a particular gentleman I should be having thoughts about?"

"No. I just…you seemed to be getting along very well with the duke."

Lady Susan frowned.

Susan knew quite well that her mother and aunt considered her of an age to marry. However, she had her own intentions, and that included enjoying no less than two seasons—three if she could manage it—before she settled to anything. She wanted balls and gowns and to be frivolous. She wanted a bit of adventure before she ended up buried in the countryside like her mother. It was all very well for Father to say Mother loved Yorkshire, with its rolling hills and reasonable access to the spa in Harrogate and the shops in York, but Susan knew just how long and dull the winters could be—and also the delight of any trip to London, a real city.

She wanted some romance in her life, by Jupiter.

But her aunt had stirred her curiosity. "Why all this interest in the duke?"

"Well, he is a duke. Does that not always stir interest?"

Susan shrugged, a gesture neither her mother nor her governess had been able to dislodge from her habits, and one Susan used when she wanted to irritate her elders just a little. "I suppose." A thought occurred. Was this perhaps about someone else's interest? She tried on what she hoped to be a dreamy smile. "He is rather handsome."

Color pinked her aunt's cheeks, and Susan decided she must pay better heed to the rest of the evening—something was afoot.

The gentlemen joined them, interrupting any other conversation she might have with her aunt, bringing with them loud voices and slightly flushed faces from their port. Davinia retired to a corner, and of course the young ladies had to entertain. Susan had a decent voice but an indifferent touch on the piano. She convinced Elizabeth and Mary they must make a trio, and she arranged it so Elizabeth would play—she showed to advantage there—and Mary would sing with her. Mary couldn't giggle whilst singing—a distinct advantage for all in earshot.

She and her friends performed three songs—only one faintly bawdy—to polite applause. Snogs—she couldn't bring herself to call her childhood friend by his title of Lord Leifmere, as if he'd become someone else in the past few months—turned the pages of the music. And Susan used the chance to watch her aunt...and the duke.

Her aunt seemed overly intent on not noticing

the duke, whist the duke's stare seemed drawn to Aunt Davinia. If she moved, his gaze followed her. If she smiled, he frowned. If she laughed—and Father and Aunt Davinia were always joking—a look of something close to longing tugged on the duke's face.

Ah, but that was interesting.

She'd heard the old stories of how Aunt Davinia had almost been snared by a duke. Or had it been the other way around? Grandmamma had always wandered off the point and into a lecture about the dangers of an idle life, how wealth and position led to a lack of consideration for the feelings of others, and would only ever give up on her tirade when Susan's father reminded Grandmamma that she might want to recall he held a title as well. That inevitably set off a row about how Grandpapa ought to have disowned the title, something Susan knew her father had said was impossible. Grandmamma had never listened to that part of the argument. Susan had become bored with those old stories ages ago. Now she wished she had listened to the context of what had been left unsaid.

Was this that particular duke? If he was, did that mean a tendré might still exist between her aunt and Everley? Just what had happened between her aunt and a duke?

Chapter Five

The snow came during the night. Piles of it.
Davinia woke to the glorious sight of ice sparkling on bare branches, of deep drifts that smoothed the landscape into a world that seemed made of whipped cream, and the sight of her breath misting the window. No one would be traveling today—not to or from Somerton. Not with roads frozen and covered in enough snow to bog the wheels of any coach. She rubbed her arms against the chill and moved to tug on the bell pull. Betty, the upstairs maid, arrived and soon had a fire reset and burning. Davinia dressed in her warmest wool gown—a pale green that at least gave the illusion of spring color—and chose a thick shawl, embroidered on both ends, for her shoulders. She even donned a lace-trimmed cap for extra warmth. She could not wait to head downstairs to seek out a snug parlor with a huge fire—and blessed hot tea. Even with wool stockings and stout boots, the drafts that seemed to slip through every window-pane and possible crack in the plaster numbed her toes. Ah, the joys of an old house. Someday, she would have herself a London residence, both smart and convenient to entertainments, with a fireplace in every room, bookshelves galore and a snug parlor that looked out onto a garden square.

Ah, the dreams of a woman without the means to see them become reality. She smiled at her folly and made her way to the breakfast room, seeking anything warm. She found her brother staring out the window in the older part of the house, which at least had paneled walls, tapestries for extra warmth, and lower ceilings.

He stood with a mug of ale in his hand. He finished it off, called for a second, and Davinia decided that could not be a good sign.

The breakfast room, paneled in dark wood, boasted only one set of windows that looked out to the front drive, a coal fire in the grate, a sideboard with warming trays and a round cherry wood table set with the second best china. It smelled of tea, toast, and rashers of bacon that left Davinia's stomach grumbling.

After seating herself and pouring her tea, she asked, "Felicity?"

Freddy's expression soured. "Still abed and insisting she has a headache coming on."

"Ah." Davinia nodded and stirred another spoon of sugar into her steaming tea. Felicity's headaches were quite famous within the family as a sign of unhappiness. Which accounted for Freddy indulging a second mug of ale for breakfast. Valentine's Day was five days off yet, but a house party with less than a handful of guests promised to be a sad affair. The ale arrived. Davinia buttered a slice of toast—already gone cold—and asked, "What do you intend to do with our guests?"

Throwing himself into a chair, Freddy shook his head. Dirt clung to his boots, his breeches hung loose as did a sturdy dark-brown coat. He smelled faintly of the stables, but that could simply be residue odor on his clothes. "I've no idea. At least young Leifmere got himself home last night. He might brave the roads on foot to return. We've Mrs. Mosby, her son, the Ambersons, the vicar, and Susan's giggling friends to look after in the meantime. And Everley." The last word came out glum.

Davinia picked up her tea, sipped, and then said, "The vicar will be happy enough in your library—you have a fine collection of books on herbs—and I dare say Mr. Amberson will be content there as well. He seemed the studious type. With luck, the older ladies may keep to their beds, particularly given that Mrs. Mosby is in the new wing and her bed will be the warmest spot to be found and Mrs. Amberson remarked on how she felt she might have a cold coming on. Susan can look to what might amuse her friends and young Mr. Mosby. Which leaves only Everley to your care."

Freddy rolled his eyes and took a long pull on his ale. "Oh, yes, and we've so much in common. He won't care to hear about my horses or my dogs, or my lands, for that matter. What in blazes does one do with a duke without a house full of guests to entertain him?"

Davinia laughed. "Honestly, Freddy, he can probably see to his own amusements. Why not turn him loose in the library with the vicar and Mr. Amberson? You can join them, and you'll have enough for a few rubbers of whist." She smiled, for she knew very well Freddy disliked any card game—too much counting up points by his reckoning.

Sitting up, Freddy put his elbows on the table. "You once had him trailing around after you in London. Repeat that magic of yours."

She put down her cup with a rattle of china, her heart beating just a little too fast. The horrid part of this was that the thought of time with Everley had warmed her. She did not want thoughts of him doing anything to her. It had taken long enough once before to try and forget him, to forget his scent...his touch. She was not about to be put in that position again. "Freddy, I had no such thing. Everley was simply—"

"Infatuated? Besotted? Dashed well ready to

propose?"

Heat scalded her skin. She took refuge in a gulp of tea, but it was far cooler than her face. Staring down into the milky depths of her tea, she fussed and smoothed the handle of the cup. "You overstate the matter." Everley had certainly taken an interest—but not the sort…well, her brother did not need to know the details. It had been bad enough that her mother had known the worst of it and that her father had shaken his head over the incident. She glanced up to find Freddy staring at her, eyes narrowed and mouth pulled down as if he was seeing more than she cared to reveal. She shifted on her seat and stirred her tea again. She needed a distraction from the topic, and she knew just how to get it. "Do you intend to remind me of all I owe you to get what you want? After all, how many brothers would take in a widowed sister and not use her poorly?"

Freddy's head came up. "I would never be so ungentlemanly as to mention such a thing." He spoilt his hurt expression with a sudden grin. "Or at least I wouldn't unless I had a thought it might work to convince you to take pity on me."

With a smile, she shook her head. "Very well. But it is for Felicity's sake, not yours, that I endure the—"

The door to the breakfast room opened, and Davinia cut off the uncharitable words she had been about to utter. Her face warmed again, for, of course, it was none other than Everley who strode in. Davinia's smile froze, and she thanked providence she had not warmed to the topic of the boredom of perfection.

If Everley had overheard any of their discussion—and why would he, given the solid oak door—he gave no sign. He greeted Freddy, gave Davinia a "good morning," and set about filling a plate from the warming trays set out on the sideboard.

The breakfast room was not so large—and the round cherry wood table not so huge—that someone might find a corner and bury himself with a newspaper. Conversation must be had. However, beast that he was, Freddy tossed back his ale, muttered a few words about estate business and fled, giving Davinia a pat on the shoulder as if she was his old hunter and in need of reassurance before facing a five-bar gate for a jump.

Frowning, Davinia decided that was perhaps uncomfortably close to the truth.

Everley sat opposite her at the round table and lifted one eyebrow. "Tea not to your satisfaction? Is your toast cold? Shall I ring for more hot water?"

Chasing away her gloom—the clouds outside provided enough of that, thank you—she managed a smile. "No...please, not on my account."

He stood anyway—and bother the man for looking so utterly marvelous. His coat in a smooth brown twill, fit without so much as a wrinkle or a crease, his cravat—unlike Freddy's hastily unmade bed, wrapped about the neck like a muffler—offered up crisp creases and delicate folds, his buff waistcoat matched breeches that clung to muscular thighs, and his boots gleamed. He did not smell of the stables. Davinia caught a whiff of soap as he moved past her to the bell pull.

A footman arrived to the summons. Everley ordered hot water, coffee, and fresh toast and turned to Davinia, one eyebrow raised. She shook her head and waved off the need for anything. Everley sat and addressed his plate of a slab of ham, bacon, and baked eggs.

Some imp prompted Davinia to ask, "What, no

conversation about the weather today?" Everley choked on a morsel of something. She almost rose to go over and thump him on the back, but hot water for tea arrived, along with coffee, which Everley poured and gulped down. He glanced over at Davinia. She bit her lower lip and then said, "Well, there *is* at least weather to discuss."

"Meaning what? You plan to delight in the very fact that we are housebound for God knows how long? All plans are overturned, and such chaos pleases you?"

"Now you're being rude."

His face flushed. "You are in the right of it. I beg your pardon."

She huffed a breath. "Oh, no—please do not go stuffy on me. Freddy's pulled a promise from me to keep you occupied as best I may, given that no other guests will arrive today, and none may leave. We are indeed stuck by a freeze that will drive us to each other's throats if this cold persists."

"You make it sound a challenge to be civil."

Her lips twitched. "It might not be for you, but it will no doubt test my skills to the upmost."

The corner of his mouth turned up—and how unfair of him that he could look a schoolboy up to mischief when he ought to look more like the stern duke she knew he must have become. *Just like his father—I must remember that unpleasant man.*

"Is that to be our entertainment?" he asked. "Seeing if we can provoke discourteous quips or a rude humor?"

She waved a hand at the quiet of the breakfast room. "Or out-and-out murder with a butter knife? That would at least enliven what has become a rather restricted house party. Of course, if you would rather,

Freddy is turning the vicar and Mr. Mosby loose in the library, and the young people might be pulled into a game of charades. Notice, too, that I do not equate you with that group of young people."

Everley paused, his coffee cup halfway to his mouth.

He was indeed here to select a bride, and therefore the prospect of spending time with the young ladies of the house ought to satisfy. Instead, he barely repressed a shudder. The thought of giggling young ladies, of vapid games to be endured, and flattery to be offered left him ready to consider the library as a possible alternative, no matter who else might be ensconced there. Or even to endure recipe swapping with Mrs. Mosby. Lord, did he even know so much as a single ingredient in anything?

Or there was Davinia—Mrs. Davenport.

She sat opposite him, her mouth curved, her eyes sparkling in a way he now recalled quite clearly. That smile, that glimmer of trouble brewing, had once ensnared him. Even now, he could feel the tug of attraction—that call to the more unsteady part of his character that he tried to suppress. Yes, it would have to be the vicar, Mr. Mosby and the library, and Lord only knew what sort of books Somerton kept. Probably stuff on agriculture, sheep breeding and tales of galloping horses and long runs on hunts of old.

But he found his mouth opening and the words spilling out. "Just what sort of entertainment do you propose for a staid, elderly fellow such as myself?"

Oh, damn and blast. He hadn't meant to ask. With the words out, he could not call them back. Davinia's eyebrows rose high, and that did it. She had as good as challenged him to endure her company. If she could do this, so could he. They'd find out who would break first and run.

Chapter Six

Davinia almost decided on the conservatory—it would be warm, after all, for Felicity had been set on forcing strawberries as well as roses. However, Everley gave her such a challenging stare, one dark eyebrow arched high as if he knew for a certainty she could not manage to behave for more than an hour. That tore it. She would show him. If he could be the perfect gentleman, she would be the perfect lady. Or almost. And Everley could dashed well enjoy the cold outside while she managed her manners.

He frowned at her choice of a tour of the gardens, which would be bare, white, and icy. She smiled and reminded him that Susan and her friends could no doubt be persuaded to offer up a few songs if he would prefer to stay indoors. Everley's expression did not change, but he rose and said he would fetch his coat, hat, and gloves and meet up with her in the main hall within a quarter hour.

Bundled into a fur-lined cloak, a muff, and woolen gloves, Davinia thought herself prepared. However, they stepped outside, and cold washed her face, stealing her breath, tingling on her skin and drying her nose. The world smelled of the fires from the house, and Davinia almost turned to go back inside to their warmth. She wiggled her toes in her boots to try and warm them.

Everley glanced at her. "Reconsidering?"

She put up her chin. "Not in the least. It is...refreshing after the stuffy house."

She thought she heard a muffled snort from him,

but a proper duke could not possibly make such a sound, and when she glanced at his face, he offered her a bland expression. He also offered his arm. She put her hand on his coat—and resisted the urge to huddle closer to his warmth.

With his hat on firm, Everley glanced at the stone steps that led up to the main house, which glinted as if fragments of diamond shards had been scattered over them. "It really is a pity Lady Somerton—your Felicity—did not think to hold an ice festival instead of a house party."

His words came out dry, and Davinia glanced at him, again, searching for some hint of humor. "Is that an actual jest you've made?"

"No, it cannot be, for I lost any sense of the absurd when the title descended upon my shoulders. However, it is a certainty that this is a ridiculous time of year to think of hosting any event this deep in the countryside."

"And yet here you are…?" She left the rest of the words dangling between them, wondering if he would admit to being here to court a wife. Could she worm from him if Susan had sparked his interest?

Everley did not answer but focused on easing them down the steps, testing for slippery ice. Davinia huffed out a breath over such caution. Letting go of his arm, she danced down the stone as fast as she could. At the bottom, standing on the pebble gravel of the drive, she looked back up at him and grinned. "Faster down, safer down. Caution on ice is for cowards, or so Freddy always tells me in the hunt field."

With a frown, Everley made his way to her side and again offered his arm. She took it, a memory stirring of his arms around her in a garden that was exploding with the heady fragrance of spring. He'd been younger—a little thinner, she thought, not quite so broad in the shoulder—and she had been...well, she'd been foolish beyond what one might expect of a girl of eighteen.

She'd been swept away. Now she had sense. She'd been married and widowed, and knew she'd been a goose to even think a duke such as him might wish for more than a temporary possession of the girl she had been. She'd been a challenge to him—nothing more. His father—and certainly Everley himself—had made that utterly clear. She glanced at him now—a sideways look—only to see him minding the path and kicking snow from the walk to expose the ice below.

Leading him with a tug, she headed for the kitchen garden, where at least something might be seen. The root crops had been mulched, and small tufts of green struggled up from straw and snow, showing leeks, carrot tops, and turnips still to be plucked from the ground. The hardiest of the herbs, such as the rosemary, fared well in tall bushes, but others looked sadly frosted and wilting. The world smelled of ice and cold and not much more. She rattled on about Felicity's plans for the kitchen garden in the spring, and tried to weave in subtle hints that Susan had no interest in anything but balls and beaus. Might that put him off the idea of Susan for a duchess?

Everley stopped and glanced down at her. She'd started to shiver, but she gritted her teeth. She would not let them chatter. Shaking his head, he started them back around the side of the house. "I'd no idea you had such an interest in flora. Do we survey the fauna next?"

She gave a laugh. "An excellent idea. The stables next."

Blessedly, they were warm. The scent of horse and leather and hay met them at the entrance. Old Seb doffed his cap, told them to mind the ice on the way back to the house, foretold more icy rain to come, and vanished into the tack room where he and the other grooms had a stove going. As Davinia suspected from the faint fumes teasing at her, they'd also added smuggled brandy to their tea. She led the way to the nearest stall. "You've met Gertie. This big fellow is Arthur, Freddy's old hunter." The tall chestnut with a huge head and wide blaze glanced at them and returned to nibbling his hay. Davinia gave him a pat on the rump and wandered down the clean-swept, dirt aisle to the far stalls. "It seems your team is now comfortably situated."

Four matched grays lifted their heads—and they certainly must be the duke's, for she did not recognize them. Everley glanced around and found his way to a feed room and a handful of grain for each horse. They swallowed up the treat and nickered for more. He scratched withers and thumped rumps and told them to mind their manners and he'd see hot bran mashes sent their way.

Davinia watched, eyebrows lifted and her hands clasped in front of her. Stepping from the stall, Everley met her stare. "What? I am a duke and so should not know my way around my own horses? I simply call for them, use them as I will, and send them away?" He gave a snort—this time she saw him do so. "I should be a poor master if I knew nothing of those in my care, including those with four legs."

She let out a breath. "Actually, it is simply that I prefer not to acknowledge that you might have a good side." He laughed, a sharp bark that seemed lacking in real amusement. She worried her lower lip with her teeth and asked, "Did I insult you? I beg your pardon."

Turning to her, eyes bright with amusement, he leaned against the stable wall. "Oh, you cannot. Not when I've been doing the same to your character. You chatter on about nothing—"

"As you did with the weather yesterday," she said, chin going up.

"Yes, we have weather and herbs and horses to discuss. Ah, Davinia, when did we set out to make ourselves into strangers?"

"That would have happened back in that garden." Face hot, she looked away and fussed with the ermine trimming on her muff. "I beg pardon...again. I seem to be doing a lot of that. But, honestly, I hadn't meant to bring it up."

"Now it is my turn to be rude, for I do not believe you. I do believe, however, that you have been wanting to throw that... that incident into my face for years. Shall we simply have the argument we should have had back then to clear this tension between us?"

She looked up at him, a breath lodged in her chest. So he felt it as well—that tug between them. Was it really nothing more than unfinished business? Was this an echo from that argument her mother and his father had had while she stared at the greenery instead of at Everley and then had bolted before she burst into humiliating tears? The embarrassment could still scorch her—that horrible moment when she'd known her mother's warnings had been nothing but the truth. With one word, she have could ruined Everley. And herself. She hadn't been able to do it.

Letting out the breath she had been holding, she glanced toward the tack room, which had gone mysteriously silent.

Everley followed her stare, gave a nod, and headed for the main stable door, which he dragged open and held for her. Cold air washed over her. She shivered but strode back into the chill.

It had started snowing again—fat, wet flakes that stuck to her cheeks and slipped down her neck, finding their way under the velvet bonnet she'd donned. The bonnet would no doubt be ruined. She took a step and slid on the ice covering the flagstone path. Everley caught her and held her steady.

Heart thudding, breath coming in short gasps, she glanced up at him. Oh, such a mistake. His face hovered close, just as it had years ago—right before he'd kissed her. Back then, he'd pressed his lips to hers without a word about love or marriage or anything proper. He'd stolen her breath, had rattled her senses, and left her wanting nothing so much as more of him.

He'd kissed her, and she'd kissed him back.

Oh, heavens, what if he did so again?

The ache rose in her chest, a sharp yearning for just such a thing. She had missed Charles, sometimes quite dreadfully. But not really as a loving wife should. She had married him very much because he stood for the opposite of everything Everley had been. Charles had been brash and rude and loud and…and, well, he'd been what her mother had wanted for her. A good common man. Everley was quite uncommon. She simply could not allow him to kiss her now and make her senses swim and leave her thoughts and emotions tumbling. She had taught herself to forget Everley. She would not go back to remembering every aching detail.

She turned away with a sudden jerk, stuffing her hands into her muff. This time at least, even if they were caught in an embrace, there could be no chance of entrapment into a marriage when all they'd really had was a mad infatuation. But she did not trust herself.

Behind her, Everley said something, his words muffled and indistinct. Davinia struggled not to look back. She did not want to see if that perfect façade of his had cracked into something far too human. Lifting her stare to the lowering sky, which had taken on the dull of pewter, meaning heavy wet hanging in the clouds, she said, "The wind's picking up. We should return to the house. I think it will snow quite hard today."

"Mind your step." Everley put his hand on her arm again.

The touch of his gloved hand drew her into making the mistake of glancing back after all. For a brief second, her gaze met his, and her heart gave a sharp twist. Oh, it could not be, but was the same longing now showing in his eyes? She must be imagining it. He could not want to make the same mistake with her again. The expression vanished, and she almost gave a laugh. She was the one in danger of repeating past errors.

She pulled away and hurried ahead, her stare fixed on the flagstone as if watching for ice when in truth she was seeing nothing. She ought to have more sense than to allow a handsome face to turn her head.

Everley caught up with her at the front steps, and still she hurried. She needed to find noise and put up some sort of barrier to that charm Everley could wield without thought. She heard a muffled curse and hesitated a fraction before putting her foot on the next step and that was her undoing. Her boot slipped on the ice, the leather bottom sliding out from underneath her.

She gave a gasp, her balance shifting. She started to fall backwards.

The next she knew, she lay partly on the cold flagstone and partly on Everley's hard, warm body, the breath half knocked from her and not just from a tumble down the steps. All she could think was, *Oh, bother—why must I be such a disaster around him?*

Chapter Seven

Oh, hell.

Everley wanted to say the words, but the air had rushed from his lungs in a sharp jab that hit somewhere on his left side. Stunned, he could do no more than try to pull in a gasp—and fail. His left ankle throbbed, and his ribs ached, but instead of doing anything about it, he stared up at a sky the color of Davinia's eyes and clung to her soft warmth.

He should let go of her. He should say something. He should get to his feet, put Davinia onto hers, and stop this from becoming another misadventure between them. Instead, he tightened his hold on her, remembering far too well how she had once softened into his embrace. She smelled of lavender, he rather thought—or was that his head swimming? The gravel of the drive pressed into his back along with the cold of a stone step against his booted leg. The stabbing in his side worsened. The sharp jolts lancing up his ankle told him he'd done something to it when he'd spun to catch Davinia. Blast all, he'd lost his hat again. He knew that, for his hair tumbled over his eyes, and the wind stung sharp on his face and head.

Trying to catch a breath, he managed one deep enough to make him wince. He gave a grunt.

Davinia shifted in his arms, jabbing an elbow into his side in just such a way that the world swam. She peered down at him, her face pale. "Oh, heavens, what did you break?"

He cleared his throat. "Nothing of account. I

seem to have landed…badly."

Muttering words no lady should know, Davinia put a gloved hand on his shoulder. "Yes, I rather think you did. Have you broken something? A rib possibly. Let us hope it is not your spine."

With a short, shivering breath, a swallow of air, he got himself up to one elbow despite Davinia trying to keep him still with one hand pressed against his chest. "It is nothing. Or at least very little." The words came out sounding worse than he'd meant with gasps between each of them. Heat pulsed into his ankle in a fashion that boded nothing good. He pressed a hand to his ribs to stop the ache there.

Davinia's gloved hand covered his. "Oh, damn."

Frowning, he put his focus on her. The world settled into better order, but that ripping pain forced his breath into shallow pulls. "If you will stand, I may do the same and we shall manage." There…he'd gotten some wind back. If he could but get himself into a comfortable chair and off this damnable ice and settled with a brandy in hand, he might very well forget this awkward closeness with her had ever happened.

Davinia glowered at him as if he were still in short pants and under her governance. "Yes, you will try to walk, won't you, you blasted man. Your stubbornness will have me swearing like a sailor."

He couldn't help it. He smiled. "I believe you have done so already."

"Well, I was married to a sea-faring fellow. If you must try to walk and will not wait for me to fetch anyone to aid you, you shall at least accept my help. Whatever were you thinking?"

To save you from such a spill.

He tried to sit upright, and that meant he couldn't

get the words out. The pain forced a grimace. He pressed his lips tight against the urge to cast up his breakfast. That would not do. A duke did not spill his partially digested meal upon a lady. He would preserve that much decorum, and he at least managed to get his back off the ground.

Davinia took hold of his right arm—he kept his left hand hovering over his side and shifted. When he could trust his feet to stay where he wanted them, he got his good leg under him, almost slipped on the ice again, and somehow made it to standing. A few shallow breaths didn't hurt all that awfully, but his left ankle was screaming now, and he viewed the steps to the front door with worry. Davinia tucked herself under his arm as if she belonged, and he was not going to dwell on the comfort of such a thing. No, he would focus only on leaning on her slender frame—that or fall down again. But this physical contact was not what either of them wanted. No—not in the least.

Her voice a tad too bright, she said, "Come now, you can do better than this. Or must I call for a stretcher? You could be carried in like a Spartan on his shield—a nobleman wounded on the goodly quest against the ice dragon of winter."

"You are not just mixing your metaphors, you are babbling them into a potpourri. I hadn't noticed you had such a quality to you."

"Babbling indeed, as if you are not. And I must. It is that or step aside and allow you to drop like a stone down a rather snow-covered well."

"You have a poor opinion of my mettle. I can manage."

"Yes, the pallor to your skin tells me as much and gives me the idea you've done yourself more harm than you will ever admit, so do not argue with me. And stop looking about for your hat. A footman can fetch it."

"I seem to be going through hats at a rather fast rate."

"You can afford a dozen new ones, and I vow if you collapse in a heap on me, I shall leave you and your hat to this wretched cold. Now, once again, gently up the steps and then to the door." They managed to get to the top, and Davinia lifted her chin and raised her voice to a shout. "I've need of some help!"

Everley winced. "So you can sound a...fishwife."

"Yes, just like my mother," she told him and shouted again.

For the moment, Everley found it difficult to focus on anything other than the next breath. He was leaning too hard against her slight frame. He pulled her closer, grabbed the smallest amount of her scent—ah, she was the lavender—and then someone had hold of him on his bad side. With a grunt, he set his glare upon a footman. But it was Davinia who spoke up. "Mind his ribs there, James. Oh, Robert, come and support him on this side. Everley, stop looking at these poor fellows as if you are about to do them harm. Your carriage accident did not put you in the ditch, but this ice did. Do stop being such a duke, for you've lost any hope of gracefulness just now, and if you go down again, I shall have these good fellows put a board under your back and carry you in as if you really are that Spartan returned from battle and not on the winning side."

That had his mouth quirking again. "I'm the least Spartan fellow about, and I do not require being carried." He straightened, kept his left arm pressed to his side, and managed with one eyebrow lifted to gain the look his father had taught him to suppress the encroachments of lesser mortals. The footmen left off trying to take his arms. They hovered like worried nursemaids with a toddler taking his first steps. The dizziness from the fall receded, and it was simply that he could not catch a deep breath without that sharp jolt of pain digging into his side, and his ankle hurt. He might well have broken something—*damnation*.

Once inside, Davinia managed to throw the house into something of an uproar. He watched her assemble more footmen and then maids. Someone was to be sent for the surgeon. That had worried glances being exchanged, and given the thickening snow outside—now dampening his hair as it melted—that seemed unwise. Everley squashed the idea with a remark about roads being impassable, which set Davinia's mouth into a mulish frown.

Somerton strolled into the main hall, glanced about, and asked in a rather irritatingly vague way if he could do anything.

Seizing the opportunity, Everley suggested a brandy and a chair. He managed to yank off his gloves, divest himself of his greatcoat without too much grimacing, all with Davinia tapping one boot, arms crossed and eyebrows raised as if she expected him to keel over. Her bonnet was wilting, and when he suggested she might wish to divest herself of her outer garments, she huffed out a breath and told him, "As soon as the weather allows, I plan to send for someone to look you over."

He started to give her a small bow—something ironic, he hoped—but checked the gesture when his ribs reminded him that such movements might be unwise. Yanking off her bonnet, leaving her brown hair delightfully tousled, she told him, "I hope it may not prove a serious injury and that you will not worsen it by being obstinate about allowing some level of care." She took herself off, and Everley worked hard not to watch her storm up the stairs.

"Was it brandy you wanted?" Somerton asked.

Everley at last got his wish for a chair beside a fire in Somerton's study, which seemed a good-sized room, blessedly warm, and near the front of the house. Everley propped up his bad leg on a footstool—the room boasted several of them, along with deep wing chairs, worn rugs that had seen much use, and plastered walls that had somehow escaped the wallpaper that decorated far too much of this house. Letting out a breath, he eyed his bad leg. He could feel it swelling and feared the boot would need to be cut off. Somerton hovered, his expression worried, and Everley finally told him to sit down and drink something. "It is not as if I am going to expire on your doorstep."

With a grin, Somerton helped them both to more brandy. "You do know Davvie's not going to let up until the bone-setter's seen you."

Everley wanted to give a snort. He settled for a sip of the brandy Somerton served—aged more than a few decades to judge by the mellow burn and the flavor of oak under the pungent aroma. "She may try. I suspect this is no more than a set of bruises." Or so he hoped. He shifted in his chair and winced.

Somerton let out a breath. "Cracked ribs, I'd say, from the way you're sitting. And we should get that boot off you. Dished myself up once like that. I'd bet Davvie I could jump the gap between our townhouse in London and the next, and I did, but only just. Smacked my side right hard into the opposite roof and had to scrabble up in such a way that it ripped my coat, ruined my boots, and didn't my mother just have a tear over all of that. Which is most likely why Davvie has the idea you've done yourself up in a similar fashion."

Sipping the brandy, Everley let the other man rattle on. The brandy and the fire wove a pleasant lassitude but could not distract from his pains. He began to think that perhaps he ought to take himself upstairs while he could. His muscles had started to stiffen.

Setting down his glass, he leaned forward to rise and found Somerton standing before him, hand stuck out. It grated, but Everley took the grip offered and hefted himself from the chair with a grunt. The world spun, pain blasted up his leg, and he sat down again, cursing.

With a shake of his head, Somerton strode to the door. Everley closed his eyes. The next he knew, his valet, Bishops, and Somerton were bent over him, with Bishops—who'd been with him donkey's years—huffing over the ruined boot. "It must come off, your grace."

For a mad moment, Everley thought he meant his leg. But Bishops straightened, left, and came back with scissors. "All of it. Boot, coat, breeches."

Everley put his hands on the arms of the wing chair. "I am not divesting myself of my garments here." Somerton and Bishops swapped looks, and Everley didn't like the somber expression on either man's face. "What in blazes do you think? I am not eighty and gout ridden!"

Somerton rubbed the back of his neck. "That leg of yours up a flight of stairs?"

With back teeth gritted, Everley struggled from the chair. "It will do." Dammit—it must. The dukes of

Everley had not come to their titles as mere courtiers but had fought beside the kings of England from Henry IV on. Even that codpiece-wearing Elizabethan rogue had taken up arms to protect his queen. Everley wasn't about to allow a bad leg to come between him and the need to climb a simple set of stairs.

He hobbled to the door, Bishops hovering close. Everley had to stop for breath and to wipe the sweat from his eyes. He admitted to himself the brandy and chair had been a mistake. He ought to have gotten himself to his rooms at once. However, there was nothing for it now but to grit his teeth and pay the price for his earlier attempt at not being an invalid.

Somehow he made it to the top of the stairs and then to the overly-decorated room he'd been given with its stripped wallpaper and fussy gilt furniture, which looked out over the back gardens. Once there, Somerton bowed himself out, saying he'd send for a doctor as soon as possible. Everley submitted to having his coat and his boots cut from his person, but he divested himself of his cravat and shirt.

"A bath, your grace?" Bishops asked.

The idea of hot water enticed. However, the thought of clambering in and out of a copper bath did not. He shook his head. "What do you have for strapping ribs?"

Somehow, Bishops managed miracles, getting Everley out of his stained breeches and his ribs wrapped with strips of linen. Where he'd gotten such things, Everley didn't ask. He did say, "I think I shall just lay myself down for a short time. Come back when it's time to dress for dinner."

Bishops bowed. "As you wish, your grace."

He left, and Everley rolled himself into bed with

a groan. And blast Davinia for being so careless as to slip—and for being right. He'd most likely broken a rib or two, or at the very least had managed to do harm to his swollen and throbbing ankle. A fine houseguest he would now make.

Chapter Eight

"I hear bones creak, your grace, meanin' a fracture to the ribs. But you're not coughing blood, a good sign. That swollen ankle, however, is of some concern. I'm thinking it might just be ligaments strained, but we'll know more once the swelling goes down. If you do not wish further damage, I suggest stayin' off your feet a goodly while."

Everley lay upon his bed, propped up by pillows. He had not been able to rise and dress for dinner, as had been his plan. He'd also been kept abed two days now with his ribs strapped, his waistcoats and coats—cut to fit exactly—unable to be coaxed into place. His foot was also swollen, meaning his shoes and boots did not fit. Unable to make himself presentable for company, he'd had to settle for meals in his room, his mood growing ever more foul, a banyan thrown over his shirt and breeches, and Bishops hovering. He had spent even worse nights, restless, hot and cold, unable to find a position that didn't leave him aching.

Somerton had stopped in this morning to warn Everley that a thaw had finally set in.

"There's mud thick on the roads, but it's possible to get across the fields, and Davvie's sent a groom to fetch Dr. Neill. Thought you should know."

Wishing for nothing so much as relief from the pain, Everley had expressed the hope that at least the doctor was competent.

"Well, he's a Scot," Somerton had said, as if that was a recommendation.

Everley found the doctor to be a brusque man,

younger than anticipated, thin with ginger coloring and his brogue tamed into a faint hint of rolling R's. Neill had prodded at his side, put an ear to Everley's chest, asked him to breathe, and looked down Everley's throat and into his eyes as if that must reveal some secrets. Perhaps it had. The man had glanced at ribs and prodded with his fingers in a way that left Everley ready to curse the fellow in a fashion that did not befit a duke.

When the doctor was done, he said, "I've laudanum I could leave, but I'm not advising it, not given that breathin' is difficult. If you can bear the pain, do so. There's not much to be done other than to allow time to knit what may mend. Rest for a fortnight at the least. Longer would be best."

Everley had been fidgeting, trying for a more comfortable way to sit upright in his bed, but now he stilled. "That is impossible. I shall remove to my house. It is only twenty miles from here."

"Two or twenty, I must caution against such recklessness. A lung puncture is possible if that rib shifts, and there's nowt any can do for you then. It'll be a full ten weeks before anything more than mild, short walks is advisable."

"I cannot trespass on Somerton for so long."

At that, Neill's pale eyebrows rose high. "On bad terms, your grace?"

"No, it is just—"

Neill turned for the door. "I'll stop again in three days to see how you fare. Send for me sooner if there's so much as a shade of pink in anything you spit up. By all means, disregard my opinion if you've no care for your well-being. I'm sure the vicar can read the rites over you." With that, he bowed himself from the room.

Muttering about quacks and their advice, Everley rang for Bishops and ordered his clothes. Bishops stiffened but did not move to obey. Everley threw back the covers and contemplated how he was to rise with his side aching and wrapped tight and his ankle a swollen, throbbing misery. He paused to catch a shallow breath and then asked, "Well, what is it now?"

"Mrs. Davenport, your grace."

"What of her?" Everley asked, a calm settling into him. "No—allow my speculation. She gave you orders to hide my clothes? To keep me abed? What foolery has she set loose now?"

Bishops fixed his stare on the opposite wall, papered in wide, gold stripes that matched the gold stripes of the chair upholstery—not a soothing color choice. "Your grace, she asked if you would care to join her for breakfast. She has ordered a meal set out in the sitting room adjacent to this. She asked in particular that I mention the coffee is still hot. She also sent this." Bishops held out an ebony cane.

The words sprang to Everley's lips to tell Bishops to toss that cane out a window. Dash it, but he could rise and dress—or he could if he stripped off the wrappings around his ribs and stuffed his foot into some sort of slipper and could do all that without a damnable hot poker plunging into his side. But…coffee? That had him pausing. Fog clung to his thoughts from two nights of poor sleep, and the lure of that hot beverage had him willing to endure small indignities.

Throwing his legs over the side of the bed, he got himself pushed to the edge. "Well, where's my banyan? I'll need slippers as well and something more than a nightshirt on my back. But a shave shall have to wait."

***

She would seduce him with strawberry jam. And marmalade, for one could not discount the excellence of cook's marmalade, a divine concoction of Seville oranges, both tart and sweet and utterly gooey. Davinia frowned at the table set for two with the rose pattern china, a plate of crumbly Wensleydale cheese, and a pyramid of oranges and strawberries from the hot house. The fresh bread and Bath buns currently had Davinia's mouth watering with their aromas, and the toasting forks stood beside the hob, ready for use with the cheerful fire.

Seduced—where had that word come from? No…not seduced. Bribed, that was more like it. Yes, she would bribe the duke with most excellent marmalade so he might obey doctor's orders and would keep his ease for a few more days at the least.

Davinia took up her cup, but she did not sip. She put it down again and fingered the gold locket she had decided to wear this morning, tucked under a lace fichu that matched the cream of her gown. She resisted the urge to stand and pace the sitting room. She had no idea if Everley would unbend enough to break his fast with her. If he did, she rather suspected he might arrive in a foul mood. Pain often did that to people. Her mother had become quite cantankerous after Father had died and as her final illness progressed. But yellow country butter and bread fresh from the oven—Felicity had persuaded Freddy into buying a new Rumford enclosed stove that was quite wonderful for baking—and delightful jam ought to provide salve to any mood Everley might bring with him.

They also might make up in small measure for Davinia having summoned Dr. Neill, no matter what

Everley might have wished.

She had overheard the doctor speaking to Freddy before Neill had departed. It was good of Dr. Neill to have ridden over on his dependable if plodding old hack, mud spattering his boots, and Freddy had said as much, but the doctor had been worried. Davinia had heard it in his tone, along with the caution of no traveling or exertion for the duke. Oh, the thought of restrictions was going to go over so very well with a duke.

Davinia pushed out a breath, dropped her locket back to nestle under her gown, and smoothed her hair. Poor Felicity's house party had been wrecked by the weather, and now Davinia had trapped Everley here with that stupid fall. Why must she somehow turn into a disaster whenever Everley was near?

Well, it was not yet Valentine's Day, and the duke was due to remain for a short time yet no matter what—but would he want to stay for as long as the doctor had advised?

A knock startled her. She sat up, but it was Felicity who poked her head around the edge of the door. "Freddy told me what you are doing, you poor dear. Do you really think this will mollify the duke and convince him that staying on with us is not such a bad thing? Should I send in Susan to help?"

Davinia blinked. "Honestly, he's just as likely to come in with more frost on him than the ground outside ever had."

Felicity came in, sat in the chair next to Davinia, and picked up a bun to butter. She looked utterly charming in a pink gown with a lace collar. She'd taken up the habit of wearing caps, this one quite fetching and trimmed in blonde lace. Small, dark, with slashes of black eyebrows over bright, green eyes, she looked more like one of the fairy folk Davinia recalled from childhood tales.

Davinia almost sighed. Where Felicity was all soft curves and grace, Davinia knew herself to be bony angles and height. She looked far too much like Freddy, both of them hardy souls from good Celtic stock somewhere back along the lineage, with brown hair and gray eyes and nothing notable about them. Felicity, with her heart-shaped face and small, curved lips, managed to make nibbling on a bun look enchanting. But the nibbling was a sign of worry.

Patting Felicity's hand, Davinia said, "Dear, I shall handle the duke until we can be certain of his mood."

Felicity put down the bun. "If the weather improves, the other guests may yet arrive, but how can I offer dancing now that the duke is injured. It will seem an insult to him."

"I don't see how that is the case. But what if the weather worsens again?" Davinia said.

With her mouth pulled into a mulish pout, Felicity shook her head. "It cannot. This will spoil all Susan's chances. Everley will remember this only as...as a horrid interval."

"Yes, that is possible. Pain does that to people. But...well, perhaps, this is a sign that, for now, it would be best for Susan to refrain from striving for any attachments?"

Felicity blinked. "A sign? I should hope I am beyond superstition. And a duke, you know, a very rich duke is nothing to turn up your nose at. I had rather hoped...well, why not a duke for Susan?"

Davinia let out a long breath. "While there may

not be an excess of dukes who are young and unattached, are you really so set upon such a match? Even if it were to bring unhappiness."

Stiffening, Felicity lifted her chin. "There is no particular reason it should do that."

Determined to make Felicity see sense, Davinia twisted in her seat to face her sister-in-law. She was far too aware how difficult it was for any young lady to resist a duke, particularly a charming one. Dukes were also used to getting what they wanted and using whatever means they needed to do so. "Come now. You've met him. Everley matched with Susan? She already thinks him too old, and he is very much set his in ways. He is…well, starched is a polite way to put it."

A slight frown creased Felicity's brow. "But, darling, he is a duke!"

"That is not an excuse for other drawbacks," Davinia muttered. She sat a little straighter and said, her tone blunt, "His wife will be a thing he owns. He probably has a list and is coming at this in the most cold-blooded way possible. I am not even certain he has seen Susan as her own person. She is simply an earl's daughter."

Felicity shook her head. "Nonsense. He noticed you once upon a time—as a person and not just as an earl's daughter."

Shooting her sister-in-law what she hoped was a fierce stare, Davinia shook her head. "That old family tale had me married when in truth there was never even so much as the mention of an engagement." Just an utter humiliation, she thought to herself. However, the turn to Felicity's mouth slipped from mulish to rock-stubborn, and Davinia knew she had pushed as hard as she might. Best to leave the seeds planted and hope

Felicity might start to see Everley as something other than a prize to be caught.

She patted Felicity's hand again. "I promise to see if I can at least coax the man into good humor and contentment to remain under your roof. I cannot do more. You have to remember this is a gentleman who came only once before this to see his nearby property, and did he pay a call upon his neighbors? No. He held one insipid ball that ended at ten with the orchestra retiring, as if he could not afford to pay them for the entire night. He served indifferent wine, and about the only good thing that might be said is that the food was perfectly wonderful. He danced with no one and returned to London the very next day."

Felicity picked up her Bath bun again. "Yes, but I do not think the ball would have ended quite so soon if you had not fallen into the fountain."

Squirming in her chair, Davinia tried for what she hoped to be a prim expression. "I didn't fall. Freddy pushed me. Well, actually, he didn't so much as push as dared me to walk the edge—on tiptoe. After a great many glasses of wine. And do not forget that was years and years ago before I'd married and become upstanding and—"

Felicity gave a snort. "Oh, fuss. Do not try to pull the wool over my eyes. But... well, will you at least promise to sound out Everley on his interest? Not this morning, perhaps, but when he is in a better frame. If he at least admires Susan, that bodes for something more promising, does it not? And there is nothing wrong with looking to Susan's future." Standing, Felicity kissed Davinia's cheek and left the room with her Bath bun.

Leaning back in her chair, Davinia grimaced. She

would be an ungrateful wretch to deny her sister-in-law anything. She knew herself to be lucky in her family. Still…Susan and Everley—she could not see it. Was she intentionally blinding herself?

Another knock sounded, this one hard and certain. Everley stepped into the room, and Davinia's eyes widened.

Oh, Susan had better never see him like this.

He didn't look a stuffy duke. He looked exotic and utterly stunning with his dark hair tousled as if he'd attempted to brush it and failed, and the scruff of a beard had started to darken his jaw. A loose robe in vibrant jewel-tone colors hung over tan breeches and white shirtsleeves. He'd left off a waistcoat. White stockings and black slippers on his feet left him proper, but he looked utterly flawed—and all too human.

Davinia's heart thudded.

This is what he looks like in the mornings—this is what I might have seen all those other mornings, if only…

And then she took in the pale skin, the tightness around his mouth and the shadows underneath his eyes. She stood and went to his side. "Heavens, you look worse than I thought you might. Did you get any sleep at all over the past two nights? I suspect not. Well, sit down. I shall pour you coffee and tempt you with marmalade and even make you toast. Do you like it light or very brown?"

He eyed the table and then her. "What, exactly, is this? Care for an invalid?"

Davinia almost let out a sigh. He sounded ready for a brawl. She shook her head. "It is breakfast and Cook's most excellent marmalade—and, I must admit, an escape for me. I am exhausted with attempts to entertain the younger guests."

"As if you are so ancient."

"Then you may think of this as something of an apology. It was my fault you fell. I was the one who slipped and took you down with me. With the benefit of hindsight, I can see that. I was cross with you for injuring yourself, but when I am the cause, I cannot maintain a temper. And...well, I did call the doctor for you without asking your permission or anyone else's. I dove in, as you have always said, without a look or a thought, and that is a poor way for me to make amends."

His frown eased. "We cannot agree. I must shoulder the blame for not only a bad landing but being so unwise as to allow you to talk me into going out of doors when I knew better."

She had to smile. "Ah, we've found a new topic to argue over. That must be better than being freezingly polite. But let us brangle over food and drink. It is at least a step more civilized. Come now, you're standing as if you'd rather not, and I cannot imagine the stairs hold any allure at the moment."

He gave a small nod, and she noted he did not attempt a bow. She got him seated at the table, the promised coffee poured, and started to slice the bread. She could feel Everley's stare upon her and glanced up to find his gaze assessing. "What? Do I have jam on my cheek? I vow I only took a small sample to assure the quality."

His lips quirked. "Why the olive branch, Davinia? What is this in truth?"

"Have I not said already? Would you care for cheese, your grace? It is a rather fine Wensleydale."

Waving the plate aside, he leaned an elbow upon the table. "I think we are far past the time when you must always use my title. What happened to us, Davinia? And, no, don't expect to pretend you misunderstand and talk of that blasted fall. Our falling out happened long ago, and I find it is something that nags at me still."

Chapter Nine

Davinia wanted to protest. He could see that in her eyes and in her parted lips that did not quite issue words. Her gaze fled to the toast on the table, to the slices she had cut, and she fumbled with the knife. He knew with a certainty she must want to do just as he had accused and pretend to misunderstand. She did not want to progress their intimacy, but now he had broached the subject, the memories poured back as if released from behind a locked door.

It had been spring, and his mother was holding some sort of breakfast in the afternoon. That much of a memory had always been with him. The house had been overcrowded and far too warm, and Davinia had taken his hand and escaped with him into the gardens—laughing of course. It had been heaven to breathe again. They'd sat on a bench amid lavender, tulips, and a riot of bluebells, the iron of the seat cold to the touch. Davinia had plucked a flower and turned to him, her mouth curving and looking lush, and her eyes bright. She had tried to tuck the bluebell into the top of his waistcoat pocket. When she failed, she had tilted up her face to his—and he had let loose those dashed impulses he'd always tired to curb.

He had kissed her.

His immediate thought had been to propose marriage—Davinia had been staring up at him, her eyes wide and something sparking in the smoky depths. A proposal ought to have come before he so much as attempted to be alone with her. He knew the proprieties, the demands of society upon himself and upon a young, unmarried lady. He could only assume a momentary madness had possessed him. A gentleman simply could not go around kissing ladies without making an honorable offer. But how could he do so? He was a Wycliffe, and Wycliffe men married at thirty. He wasn't even twenty-six, and here he was caught in the very trap his father had warned him against—a trap he'd evaded for years. He'd ignored other young ladies who had thrown out lures. He'd managed mothers intent on pushing their daughters into his path. Why was Davinia different? Why had he kissed her? Well, that had no longer mattered. He'd been caught between his duty to his family and what he owed to her reputation.

 He'd tried to organize his thoughts, but he had no idea what to say. *This is impossible. We must forget this happened. Can you forgive me?* Except he had wanted to kiss her again. He'd drawn back with an apology already forming in his mind, but he couldn't recall if he'd said anything. However, the spark had fled Davinia's eyes—he remembered that. Her smile had vanished. Then the entire mess blew up like an ill-primed pepperbox exploding in the hand, scattering the pistol and powder over everything.

 Davinia's mother had stormed into the garden, had taken one look at him still holding Davinia's hand, and launched into a vulgar condemnation of rogues with a title and nothing more to offer, muttering how France had it right in lopping off such heads. That had set off his temper. He'd stood, had said something cutting—he couldn't recall what now, but it had to do with lowbred viragos. Davinia—with a gasp—had stood as well and pulled away. And then, of all things, his father had come upon the wretched scene and set to with Davinia's parent about attempts at entrapping a man into marriage all for the sake of gaining a title. At that point, Davinia had wisely fled.

Davinia looked very much as if she wished to bolt again. She was avoiding his stare, trying to look anywhere but at him, trying even harder to get the bread onto a toasting fork and succeeding only in making crumbs.

He took the bread and knife and set about cutting better slices. "No wish to revisit the past? Perhaps you are in the right about that. It is long ago and over and done with." She glanced up at him, her mouth flattened and a look of caution in her shadowed eyes, as if debating some withering remark. Before she could say anything, he leaned back and winced. "I seem to excel at bringing you distress."

After making a face, she took the toasting fork from him and set the bread next to the flames. "Dark or light?" she asked, her back stiff. She pressed her mouth into a line.

"You shall catch that on fire if you hold it so close."

She angled a glance at him. "It wouldn't be the first thing I've burnt."

"Are you speaking of bridges and myself?"

She gave a laugh then and checked the toast. "Must everything be about you, Duke?"

"Of course. Not only am I duke—as you like to remind me—I can at the moment claim an invalid's right to excessive consideration."

"Ah, you have discovered the advantage to your situation. I urge you to make the most of it while you can. And now the toast is done." She set about buttering it with a will, and Everley could only wonder if any would be left to eat.

"I wrote you," he said.

She glanced up, the butter knife stilled. "Yes, I know. Two very proper letters full of…of well, propriety. Mother burnt them after we read them." Everley's face warmed. He'd meant the letters for Davinia only. He had wanted to salvage something between them. Davinia went on slathering marmalade over her toast. "She held herself to blame that she had allowed me such a loose rein in town. She didn't want to confess anything to Father. And, of course, she blamed you for being a duke first and not much of a gentleman second."

Everley stiffened, heat under his skin. "Is that why you gave me the cut direct on Oxford Street?"

Cheeks pink and evading his gaze, Davinia asked, "Butter only? Or will you try Cook's marmalade? I give you fair warning, however, if you do not leave off on this topic, I might be forced to upend the pot over your head." She looked up from her toast and fixed a stare on him. "Mother was shopping with me when I saw you last. I'd been mortified once, and another public embarrassment seemed…well, there was nothing to say, was there? Think of it more as a kindness that I looked away without acknowledging you."

Frowning now, Everley resisted the urge to drum his fingers on the table linen. "I thought you wanted me to leave off the topic. No, please do not torture another slice of bread." He rose, shifted his chair with more difficulty than he liked, and took up the toasting fork. "Besides, given your expression just now—and the threat of marmalade in my hair—I would just as soon have any weapons far from your reach."

A smile softened her frown. "You are a

provoking man, and I ought to skewer you. I thought if I satisfied your curiosity, we might progress from turning up old ground to a discussion of what might amuse you while you are trapped with a bad leg and worse ribs. Do you read?"

Everley secured a slice of bread on the fork and set it to toasting. "I assume you mean novels and not that I have a servant to do something so lowly for me as to sift through all my correspondence," he said, blithely ignoring the fact that he had a secretary just for that purpose. "I have been known to enjoy a good work of fiction."

"But poetry gives you a headache?" she asked, a smile lurking in her eyes. "I could bring you selections from Freddy's library." Leaning back, she recited, "*The Life and Strange Surprising Adventures of Robinson Crusoe, Of York, Mariner: Who lived Eight and Twenty Years, all alone in an un-inhabited Island on the Coast of America, near the Mouth of the Great River of Oroonoque; Having been cast on Shore by Shipwreck, wherein all the Men perished but himself. With An Account how he was at last as strangely deliver'd by Pyrates* is available. His plight was far worse than yours, so that should be uplifting. Or perhaps *Gulliver's Travels, or Travels into Several Remote Nations of the World. In Four Parts, By Lemuel Gulliver, First a Surgeon, and then a Captain of Several Ships*, which is a favorite of Freddy's and much worn. Or if you care for Maria Edgeworth we have both *Castle Rackrent* and *Belinda*, but I will say I prefer the satire and adventure in Rabelais' *La vie de Gargantua et de Pantagruel*—one of the more ambitious earls managed a translation into English that is almost as humorous as the original French. And if not books, what about games? There should be a board for something or other somewhere in the house. I won't offer chess, for I'm horrible at it."

"That is a recommendation. You could allow me to beat you soundly."

"Which would bore you within an hour."

Everley gave a nod of agreement and wondered how it was that she knew him so well. He allowed her to ramble on about possible entertainments—some of them sounding ghastly, what with skittles offered, or Snakes and Ladders, or perhaps when Everley felt up to coming downstairs a rubber of whist could be had. At that, Everley glanced down at his undress and back up to Davinia. "I shan't be going much of anywhere until I can leave off these da—devilish wraps. Nothing fits." She had been sipping her tea and gave a snort and had to cover her mouth to avoid an ungainly spitting out of the beverage. Everley chose to keep the high ground and simply raised an eyebrow. "I fail to see the humor in that."

"Oh, I was just picturing you in one of Freddy's loose coats. Actually, that might do. He's broader about the chest and waist. It won't be fashionable, but it would make you presentable—or as fit as possible—for polite company."

Giving a thought to a long dinner, to having to turn to address his neighbor on either side of him, of having to then get through port and tea after, Everley let out a breath. "Thank you, but your brother may keep his own clothes."

She gave a shrug, told him she must go and see if Susan needed her, and asked if she might send his valet to him. Everley declined the offer, but after she had gone, he made for his room and his bed again—and cursed his ribs, his throbbing ankle, and Davinia for again starting to make his life far too complicated.

***

Davinia made good on her promise to bring Everley books. A stack of them. More correctly, she sent them to him via a footman. A backgammon board followed, but it was missing a piece. Everley had his valet blacken a shilling to use in its place and set up the board in the sitting room. A package arrived after that, neatly done up with string and paper. The attached note held Davinia's slanting hand and simply said, *You'll look awful, of course, but think of the comfort. Besides, you are a duke and so above reproach no matter what you do or wear, so perhaps you will be starting a new fashion.*

He found enclosed a black coat, a double-breasted bottle-green coat, and two waistcoats, one a decent brocade and the other boasting broad yellow stripes. Bishops almost dropped the tray he was carrying that held 'a little something' sent up by Lady Somerton. The cup rattled in its saucer, the stacks of cold meats, cheeses, and cakes wobbled, and Everley shot Bishops a glance.

Face pale, Bishops settled the tray of afternoon refreshments on a side table. "Your grace, you cannot be considering wearing..." He lost his words and was left to gesture at the offending garments as if snakes must soon crawl out of the sleeves.

Everley glanced from the coat and waistcoat to his valet. His mouth crooked. "It seems, as a duke, I may wear what I wish."

"Your grace, the question remains *why* would you care to wear those items?" He made the last word into a complaint and a sneer, with a haughty wave at the striped waistcoat.

"Because it is a gauntlet thrown down." He threw off his banyan and winced but stated, "I shall dress for dinner."

Chapter Ten

She'd thought Everley would look absurd in Freddy's too-large coats and that garish stripped waistcoat. Freddy thought the garments all the crack but had yet to wear them, which was why he had donated them to her cause. However, she found she had to give Everley his due. The force of his personality was such that one noticed him and not so much his clothing. He managed to carry off the slightly loose black coat and that rather eye-catching waistcoat with aplomb, even if his cravat was not quite perfection. She told him as much when she met up with him in the drawing room before dinner.

"You may even set a new style," she said. "Why not add the cane for distinction?"

Everley cocked a disdainful eyebrow. "On the street, a walking stick is invaluable. I can manage well enough in Somerton's house without such an affectation." He moved off to pay his respects to Freddy, who had been in a conversation with Mr. Amberson, and Davinia started to wonder if perhaps she had it wrong about his being in the market for a wife. Oh, he certainly did his duty by the young ladies, with a bow here, a nod there, and a civil word for everyone. However, he seemed to regard the young ladies with tolerance rather than interest tonight. Or perhaps it was just that his ribs were aching.

Dinner went off well enough, although Felicity's conversation was perhaps a touch too bright. She worried about the now mud-bound guests and if more might arrive before Valentine's Day. Weather was certainly the topic on everyone's mind, that and asking after Everley's health until the man must be heartily sick of an overabundance of consideration. Davinia kept watch on him, and when she thought his face a touch too pale and his lips pressed thinner than usual, she dropped a word in Freddy's ear. "Do manufacture some excuse to pull him into your study for some of our grandfather's good brandy and a seat by your fire."

"What am I to invent?" Freddy asked and frowned.

"Everley collects first editions—or he used to. Use that. You don't have to produce the book, just the brandy."

Freddy gave her a sideways glance, but Davinia noticed he did as she'd asked, for when the gentlemen came in after their port, Freddy and Everley were not with them, and the vicar muttered something about books in the study. Tea was served, and Susan brought a cup to Davinia. "I am given to understand the duke must have you to thank for his comfort."

Taking up her cup, Davinia stirred the steaming liquid that held the musky notes of a strong black tea and ignored the conversational gambit. "How are your friends surviving the enforced house party? Has anyone yet suggested rolling up the carpet for dancing? We might manage four couples if the vicar and Mr. Amberson participate. Mrs. Amberson might be called upon to play something."

"I thought the topic was the Duke of Everley?" Susan folded her hands primly in her lap. "Father said he's got you looking to the duke's entertainment. Is that progressing well?"

Davinia gave her niece a hard stare. "You are persistent. Do you have an interest in that quarter?"

Susan smiled. "I simply ask after one of our guests. But I will venture to say that it does seem as if there is a...well, shall we say, a certain something between the two of you."

"Yes, it's called animosity." She put her teacup and saucer on a side table. "Or, no, that is too strong a word. We are just opposites."

"Is that such a bad thing? Perhaps he is the stability for you, and you are what he needs to keep from becoming a dull stick."

Davinia gave a laugh. "If you speak of your elders in such a fashion in your mother's hearing, you are going to give her the vapors. She will think she's raised an unnatural, wild child. Why would you think him a stick—dull or otherwise?"

"You were not seated next to him at dinner as was I. He had little conversation, or perhaps it was that he was more focused on what Mr. Amberson was saying that amused you."

Davinia leaned closer. "Or perhaps it was that his injuries pain him, and he was wishing he'd kept to his bed for another few days. He looked a touch peaked to me, but the man never will admit to the flaw of being human."

Brows arched high, Susan said, "You know him well then to make such an observation."

Skin warm, Davinia rose and shook out her skirts. "I think I must rescue your mother from Mrs. Mosby, who seems intent on obtaining every recipe Cook has." She crossed the room to where Felicity had been trapped on a small sofa. In truth, she wished more to escape Susan's prying than she did to insert herself into any conversation with Mrs. Mosby. Davinia knew little about cooking and even less about recipes.

However, a discussion of the merits of basil over tarragon or the judicious use of thyme in soup seemed an excellent way to not think about Everley.

Oh, she could tell herself she was simply preoccupied with him because he'd been injured on her behalf and required care, but their earlier conversation had left her unsettled.

She did not want to remember his letters and did not want to think that it mattered to him that she had turned away from him on Oxford Street all those years ago rather than endure the potential for yet another scene with him. She'd also been angry at the time. Angry and embarrassed that she'd been caught kissing him without so much as the mention of an engagement. She had wanted only to escape from his sphere. Her mother had obliged with a trip to Bath and then down to Lyme Regis. She'd met Charles Davenport there, but he had been focused upon his career and had not taken up a courtship until a year and a half after that. By that time, her father had passed, Freddy had come into the title, and Mother had greeted Charles as something of a savior for Davinia.

Davinia was certain she'd been the bane of her mother's life. She considered herself plain as leather, and her manners...well, Mama had done the best she could, but at times Davinia sorely felt like what she was—the daughter of a merchant's daughter.

At least Charles hadn't minded her lack of feminine graces.

One day we'll have a sloop, and I'll take you aboard as my first mate. You'll be a bonny first mate!

Davinia smiled at the memory, thankful it no longer lodged so much as a pang in her heart, and pulled herself back to the present. It was a match for

Felicity's daughter she must consider. However, neither Everley nor Susan seemed the least interested in such a thing. Well, she would just have to make certain such a condition continued to prevail.

***

Felicity threw herself into decorating for Valentine's Day—it was now only a day off—and she drew everyone she could into planning games as well as selections for the dinner menu. Mrs. Amberson seemed delighted to take on the task of deciding what dishes best celebrated a day dedicated to a saintly man and to love. The vicar promised a recitation of sonnets and retired to the library to make his selections. Susan drew the younger people into making valentine cards from cut paper, lace scraps, and ribbons. Freddy escaped with his dogs, taking Mr. Mosby and Mr. Amberson with him to brave the chill wind and telling everyone they had hopes of bagging a couple of braces of ducks. Davinia left the duke with a stack of books to entertain himself.

Not an hour later, Everley—bored beyond anything—made his way into Freddy's study. He had tied his own cravat and managed something worthy of the country but rather embarrassing for the city. Freddy's loose black coat did not make too many demands upon him, and the more reasonable of the borrowed waistcoats did not restrict his breathing. He found Davinia sitting behind a vast, ancient oak desk with what seemed like account books spread out, a quill in her hand, and a crackling fire going in the hearth. With the thick rugs and book-lined walls, the room made for a snug retreat on what was otherwise a gray day outside of the house. Everley bowed and offered an apology for disturbing her. "I was in search of your brother."

Stretching, Davinia waved him into the room. "Do come in before Felicity takes note that I am not arranging flowers."

Everley paused, glanced behind him, and then shut the door. By rights, he ought to continue his search for his host. However, what he really ought to be doing was to be seeking out the young ladies and making a selection for a wife. That idea did not seem as tempting as time spent with Davinia. As usual, she was leading him from his duties and the path that ought to be clear before him. She had snared his curiosity. "Flowers?" he asked.

Leaning back in her chair—a stiff, high-backed affair, heavily carved and large enough to make her seem small—she wrinkled her nose. "It is a task I enjoy in summer when there are actual flowers, but really there's not much greenery to be had just now. It is mostly a matter of pushing a few roses into place and adding whatever leafy, green thing that can be had in February. Please, if you were hoping for some of the brandy, do take a glass." She gestured to a seat, but he only came closer to the desk and glanced down at the papers.

Craning for a view, he asked, "Account ledgers?"

"Freddy's always been rotten at anything to do with numbers. I take far more after my mother's side of the family in that I seem to have an affinity for dealing with money." She said the words with something of a challenge, her chin lifted and a dare for him to say anything about her mother's background in trade.

Everley was not about to rise to that bait. He simply nodded and put a finger down on a column. "Does the estate really make so much profit from wool?

I shall have to ask my steward why we cannot do so well."

"Ah, now you have hit upon where Freddy does excel. You would think he was born in the North Country and not London-bred. He's purchased rams from both Bell of Dalton and Maynard of Ereyholme and has been doing very well with crossing Swaledale ewes and Bluefaced Leicesters. The offspring are prolific and hardy."

Smiling, Everley lowered himself into a chair opposite the desk. His duty could wait for a bit. "I knew if I came this far from London I should end up discussing sheep."

Taking up her quill, Davinia addressed herself to the ledgers. "Yes, well, that is what one does when in Yorkshire. Freddy is an avid follower of Robert Bakewell's work on livestock and his 'in-and-in' breeding."

She meant to bore him into leaving. He felt certain of it. However, he had a small advantage. Shifting his position to a more comfortable one, he stretched out a leg toward the fire. "Ah, you mean Bakewell's New Leicester rams. Sadly, I've been dealing with the gift of eight Merinos—a royal gift and as temperamental as any group of princesses. Prized wool they may have, but they seem to pine for the heat of Spain. The least chill of an English day, and they lose weight and will not lamb."

She glanced up, surprise in her eyes, but that was soon replaced by a teasing sparkle. "Why have you not thought to build them a hothouse for their palace? They could be like Felicity's roses and forced into bloom. I can see them now—white upon green in a lovely, huge glass house."

He gave her another smile. "I think I would rather see about crosses with some Cheviots."

She blinked, and her mouth fell open. His glance went to that mouth, and he had to look away before he started to think of those warm, soft lips. After clearing his throat, he said, his tone only slightly unsteady, "I fear I am fully rusticated. I've been reduced to tomes on horticulture and shall no doubt end up with a moniker such as Turnip Tounsend if I stay much longer in these northern wilds."

That surprised a laugh from her. "I don't know what could be used with Everley—Ewely Everley?"

Glancing at her, he gave a shudder. "Anything but that. You must save me from such a fate. I could have the backgammon board brought down. Or Freddy has a chest set here—a rather nice one. I could teach you the game." She spread her hands over the account books, but he interrupted before she could make an excuse. "Come now. You cannot claim ledgers are better company. Besides, I provide a far better excuse to avoid Valentine's duty should Lady Somerton come in search of you."

She pulled a face but rose from behind the desk. "Well, if you intend to pull rank, I must give in. However, we both shall need fortification." She brought over the chess table, poured two glasses of brandy, and settled in the opposite chair. Everley began with a brief explanation of the game, how the pieces moved, and started into strategy. Davinia's glass was already half empty and she waved her hand for him to get on with it. "I shall learn better if we play."

She learned fast, and after two more glasses of brandy—and three rapid defeats—she managed to at least capture his queen. Leaning back in her chair, brandy glass in hand, she said, "Lud, this game is far too like war. I think I prefer the account books."

He shook his head. "You are too rash a player. You must learn to plan your strategy."

Head tipped to one side, she asked, "Is that the lesson this game taught you? Life is all plans and strategy, and never should you act without thought? What of feeling and the exhilaration of an action taken without calculation? What of following instinct?"

Everley busied himself with resetting the pieces. They were straying onto dangerous ground. He could feel it. But he had matched her drink for drink. The brandy and the warmth of the room loosened his tongue, and he couldn't hold back the words. "A duke cannot afford such luxuries."

She gave a laugh. "A rich duke such as yourself can afford anything. It seems more a matter of won't. Have you never thought that even an attempt at fun is far more enjoyable than the rigor of responsibility?"

Pushing up from his chair, he took a breath and came around to her side. He reached for her glass. "I think perhaps you have had a touch too much."

She drained her glass and gave it to him. "Or not enough. I'm pleasantly tingly but still have all my sense, and as you note, I am a rash player. So I shall plunge on and ask, did you come to Somerton to find yourself a wife?"

He had been putting down the glasses. He paused and then settled them carefully on the silver tray. "Rash indeed. Such a move on the chessboard might cost you a knight or a rook at the least."

"You don't answer, which means of course you did. Pray why now? I thought you must be a confirmed bachelor."

Turning, he faced her. "Thirty is a perfectly good age at which to marry."

She laughed, a hearty and musical sound that set his teeth on edge. Sitting up, she said, "That is absurd. Why not twenty—or forty? Do you really mean to marry for no better a reason than an age set upon you? Or is it simply that thirty is the age when all dukes marry? Or when *you* must marry. And why is that? And if you think it such an excellent age, why ever did you kiss me in that garden? Oh, but I know the answer to that one. You did not intend marriage with the likes of me."

Stung, stomach knotting, he stiffened. "You cannot resist picking at it, can you? I do not know what I intended that day, which makes it an excellent example of rash action landing one in the briars."

Her face reddened. "Now I am the briars?"

"Come now—you must admit an alliance between us would have been unbearable. Your mother would have hated my family even more than mine would have scorned yours."

Her tone sharpened, and she gave a harsh laugh. "Ah, but you now consider an alliance through my niece. How kind of you to shift your position and to not think of Susan as briars. Is the taint of trade now diluted enough to suit your exacting standards? If I had known your expectations were so very high, I would have done my best never to cross your path."

Heat scorched through him. He tightened one hand into a fist and fought to bite back the anger that surged, but her words cut far too deep. "Mrs. Davenport, you have convinced me that you are in the right of it—that would have been the best for us both. You have pointed out the obvious. Any alliance that would bring our families in closer contact would not be advisable since it would bring us into each other's company. You may be certain I shall not trouble your niece with attentions that must cause a rift between her and yourself. Good day, madam." With that, he strode for the door, hardly seeing where he was going, the heat still on his skin as if she had flayed him, and wishing he had never even thought to come to Somerton.

***

Deflating, Davinia fell back into her chair. She put cold hands to her hot cheeks. She had what she had wanted. Everley had just vowed not to court Susan. Why did she not feel better about her victory?

Oh, heavens, what will Felicity think?

She pushed aside the thought, for another had occurred. How was she ever to face Everley again after enacting such a scene? She might claim the brandy had gone to her head. However, she knew herself to be quite sober—horribly so. She had been reckless. He had the right of it. She could not resist digging into that old scene that lay between them, rubbing at it as if it was a wound that continually ached. She must fuss and fuss, and seeing him had made it all the worse. Folding her hands in her lap, she pulled in a breath. She had ruined Susan's chances with Everley, that was certain. Even worse, she had insulted a guest in her brother's house and had acted in such a fashion as to confirm every poor opinion he must have of her. She must find a way to make this right—to make amends. But how?

Standing, she strode to the fire and stared into the faltering embers. She would have to learn from Everley—drat the man. She would have to plan some sort of strategy.

Chapter Eleven

His first instinct was to ring for Bishops, have his bags packed, call for his carriage, and leave this place before another hour could pass. Limping up the stairs and into his room left his side aching, his ankle throbbing, and his temper in shreds. He wanted to storm up and down the room. He wanted to call for a horse, jump on its back, and gallop to anywhere else. He wanted to descend back down those stairs to Davinia and indulge in some rather satisfying yelling that did not befit his station and which would have left his father horrified at such an outburst.

Damnation, but that woman got under his skin.

He could not account for it. Leaning a hand against the mantle of the fireplace, staring at the unlit kindling, he let out a low growl. He should not have allowed her words to incite him—but he had. He had taken offense at her scathing tone, and that laugh she'd given when he'd said thirty was a good age to marry had been the start of it.

He should not care. It should not matter to him if she thought it an absurd notion to follow a family tradition that had been ingrained in him, but it did. His temper began to cool, and still he could see no escape from remaining under the same roof as Davinia. He was a guest of Somerton's, a gentleman, and a Wycliffe. He must master this urge to lure Davinia into an argument that would bring down the house. He would not indulge in rash actions, as he'd just accused Davinia of doing. He would manage to do what he always did—he would see to his duty.

With a grimace, he limped to the bell and tugged hard to summon Bishops. He was also going to bathe, start wearing his own clothes, and hang these blasted ribs and his throbbing ankle. Dancing might still be beyond his capabilities, but Davinia had thrown down the gauntlet. He would attend this blasted Valentine's ball tomorrow night if it killed him. He would show her an unruffled façade, and he would pray for a fast healing and that he might find one of the other candidates for duchess appealing enough to wed so he could be done with this uneasy feeling Davinia had left in his soul.

***

The least he could have done, Davinia decided, was to come downstairs in a temper. Or, if he had put on pompous airs, she could have felt far better about their brangle. She would have been able to apologize and either lure him from his displeasure or puncture his arrogance with a few pithy remarks. Instead, she had nothing to either break or mend. She found it inconsiderate of him that he prove himself the perfect gentleman, for it put an itch under her skin to act an utter shrew in his presence.

The man was an outrage. Yes, that applied. How dare he stand at the piano, turning the sheet music as if nothing else mattered. Mrs. Amberson, who sat at the keyboard, glanced up at him from time to time, smiling like a smitten girl of seventeen. Why wouldn't she, with the duke oh so handsome in his black tailcoat, black breeches, white stocking and shirt and cravat, a cream-colored waistcoat embroidered finely with silver and blue threads, and black pumps. He looked a pattern card, with his hair a perfect sheen of black. One could almost miss the fact that he favored one leg—his ankle was no doubt throbbing from him being on it for so long. He winced only occasionally when he had to lean to turn the page. Well, blast the man.

The talk at dinner had been of the ball tomorrow, with everyone speculating on if the moon would still be full enough for travel, and if the roads would be frozen enough without being too iced, and if the weather would hold clear but cold. Davinia had no chance of a word with Everley, despite several attempts to single him out. Instead, Susan hung on his arm, laughing bright, teasing him from his mood in a fashion that Davinia knew to be well beyond her abilities. She could almost dislike her niece.

She also began to wonder if Susan had set her sights on the duke, despite his vow to avoid any alliance between the families. She had no chance to ask Susan the question. The house had filled with guests who had traveled north to attend Felicity's ball, and Davinia was feeling a touch *de trop*—very much the widowed relative who had no purpose here. Freddy at least sought her out after dinner, saying, "Why so glum, old thing?"

She pulled a face. "I do feel old. Old enough to be slightly tarnished." She huffed out a breath and pulled at the fringe on her shawl. "I picked a fight with Everley."

"Ah—and can't think what to do about it?" he asked.

Glancing up at her brother, she studied him. He stood there, his usual faint smile in place, slightly rumpled even in his fine evening clothes. She folded her hands in her lap. "What would you do?"

"Oh, it's easy for gentlemen. It's either a glove in the face and a duel next morning or we just pretend the other fellow don't exist."

She gave a laugh. "I can't do either of those things."

"Then just beg his pardon."

"I have been doing that the entire time he's been here," she said.

"Ah, well, that settles it. It must be love." He gave her a rather fatuous smile.

Wanting to stick out her tongue at him, she curbed that urge and asked, "Why would you say such a thing? Really, Freddy, you're no help at all, mocking the situation. Now, I believe I shall retire. I have the headache. Please make my excuses for me." She rose from her seat and strode away, but not before she heard a snort from her brother and muttered words she did her best to ignore, for they sounded suspiciously like, "Love it is."

***

Davinia fretted over what to wear to Felicity's ball. She also could not decide whether Everley was avoiding her or if she was somehow managing not to find his whereabouts. He had not come down to breakfast—she knew that for she had waited to pounce on him. She'd spent two hours that morning struggling over a note that might convey heartfelt remorse for her words and yet not come across as groveling. She had failed the task. Felicity had managed to drag Davinia into last minute worries over if the quartet hired to play that night would arrive, and if there would be sufficient food for a late-night supper. She had also torn Davinia's peace to shreds, what with looking out the windows every five minutes, fretting over the clouds scudding fast on an easterly wind, and her remarks on how the duke seemed out of sorts. Avoiding that topic, Davinia had fled to her rooms with the excuse of wanting to rest before the evening's festivities.

Settling at last on a rust-colored gown, heavily embroidered about the hem and bodice in gold and cream, with long sleeves and a square neckline, Davinia dressed. Betty managed to coax a few stray curls into Davinia's hair with a pair of tongs heated in the fire, but Davinia could not sit still for more. The pearls also did not match, so she left them off and settled for earrings of amber and a matching bracelet over her long, white gloves. At the last minute she added her gold locket with its pressed and dried bluebell, hoping it might act as a talisman against any more social gaffs. She carried a Kashmir scarf draped over her arm and a painted silk fan hung from her wrist by a ribbon. She had hoped to have a word with Everley in the drawing room before dinner, but Susan and her friends already had the duke cornered, and Susan insisted on going in on Everley's arm.

The dratted man also met the speaking glances she sent his way with eyebrows raised, as if he could not understand her meaningful gaze. That set her temper on edge. She touched the locket—a good reminder of how things could get out of hand—and tried to enjoy the evening.

More guests arrived—all locals, happy for any excuse to exchange gossip and find entertainment. The carpets had been rolled up and carried away to make room for dancing, the floors chalked in pretty patterns to keep dancers from slipping on the polished wood, and the quartet provided lively tunes. The rooms filled with chatter, laughter, the honey-scent of the candles, and a mixture of perfumes and the scent of Felicity's roses. Davinia found herself starting to enjoy the evening.

By eleven, her feet ached from standing, her forced smile had faded, and she had given up on Everley. She found a settee in the far corner of the drawing room and closed her eyes—only for a moment, she told herself. A bounce of the cushion next to where she sat pulled her eyes open.

Felicity sat next to her and let out a long breath. "I declare defeat," she muttered. She waved over a footman, took two of the wine glasses, and offered one to Davinia. "This is the last of the hock. Freddy would not hear of dealing with the gentlemen of the coast for smuggled goods, given that the war with France drags on and on. Do you think anyone has missed champagne? We shall have to manage with punch for the rest of the night."

Turning her wine glass in her hands, Davinia said, "The music is bright. The drawing room is crowded enough, for the weather cooperated, and a sufficient quantity of the local gentry attends. I should think you would be declaring this a victory. Who else has managed a ball in February? Oh, and you have a duke in attendance."

Felicity wrinkled her nose and sipped her wine. "That is the defeat. Susan has informed me she intends to accept Leifmere—eventually. She wants two seasons at the least, three preferably, and how she will keep that poor boy dangling after her for so long, I have no clue about. The duke's invitation was all for naught. Only just look, she is giving the card she made today to Leifmere."

"She might yet also change her mind," Davinia said.

Turning slightly on the settee, Felicity shot a frown at Davinia. Felicity looked lovely in a blue gown, decorated down the front with a leaf motif. "You say that as if you've no idea of your niece's disposition. She is far too like you and Freddy—amiable to a point and then stubborn as a sow in slop who will not be moved."

Davinia gave a low laugh. "Oh, unfair to compare your own daughter—and husband—to farm animals. And me as well."

Waving a gloved hand, Felicity said, "You're all cut from the same cloth—quite set in your ways and slyly proud of it. How else do you think Freddy wore me down enough to convince me to marry him—and convince my family. He was only the son of a younger son back then. I don't even think you were out of the schoolroom when he started courting me. He had no prospects. My mother took to her bed when she heard of his wishes, and my father forbade the match."

Davinia smiled. She had heard the story before but saw no reason to stem Felicity's recollections. Felicity might have on a cap—quite a frothy thing with lace—but she looked very much a girl as she gazed across the room to where Freddy stood by a table that had been carried in for him to make punch.

The drawing room stood at the back of the house and provided room for dancers as well as the pianoforte. Two knots of the elderly guests, in rather dated satin and lace, sat in chairs to observe the festivities, while Freddy held court with the squire, the vicar, and three other gentlemen. It was not the sort of exalted company Everley must regularly encounter in London. Davinia shot him another glance. No, he still had on that fixed smile as if he would never admit country society to be inferior—or rather boisterous, given the young people laughing now as they exchanged the cards they had made earlier in the day.

Nudging Davinia's elbow, Felicity asked, "What should we do? With the duke, I mean. Now that Susan has declared her intentions, I've no use for him, but you seem to have gone from living in his pocket to avoiding him in just one day. By what Freddy said, the doctor says the duke must stay with us another week at the least."

Face hot, Davinia stared into her golden wine. The fumes wound up to her, sweet and somewhat tempting, but she feared it would taste of vinegar, given her sour mood. She put back her shoulders and faced Felicity. "We argued. That is to say, I—"

"You needled him until he lost his temper?"

Davinia clenched her fingers around her wine glass. "Why do you put this on me? Am I at fault because a duke certainly cannot be?"

Leaning forward, Felicity said, her voice low, "Darling, you know very well if an argument occurred, it did so because you were being provoking. I could not ask for a better sister, but I have seen you go after Freddy just so, seeking such a row. From what Freddy has told me, your mother would have done better by the both of you to have read fewer moralizing sermons and put more effort into teaching you such things as how to curb the impulse to blurt out any and every thought."

Blinking, Davinia could only stare. With a smile, Felicity leaned back against the brocade cushions. "But there it is. Your father was too preoccupied by his artistic friends, and your mother had no idea. It is no doubt due to her mother having died young. It leaves a terrible hole in one's education. I should be very angry with you, of course, if Susan had not made up her mind to have Leifmere."

"Thank you for not being angry. That does not, however, help deal with the issue of having to endure an overly polite duke for another week."

Standing and shaking out her skirts with one hand, Felicity said, "That is just what I mean. Only you would see politeness as a problem. The issue is to find entertainments for him. Now you must excuse me. Freddy has the vicar grinning from only one cup of punch, which means it is deathly strong and will have the entire room falling down drunk if I do not get Mercer to thin its potency." She hurried away with a soft swish of silk to see her butler.

The dancing had paused for a natural break for the musicians. The duke escorted Mrs. Amberson to the punch. If it was as strong as Felicity feared, it might well loosen up the duke's proper manners—along with everyone else's. Davinia saw Susan momentarily alone and made her way to her niece, abandoning her wine glass en route. Linking her arm with Susan's, Davinia said, "Take a turn about the room with me, will you?"

Head tipped to one side, Susan asked, "Is this about the duke? I saw you and Mother with your heads together. Have you come to tell me I am too young to know my mind? That I should not decide upon anything until I have seen more of the world and met more gentlemen?"

"Is that what your mother said? And here she was lecturing me on holding my tongue. She ought to know such a conversation is bound to make you do the opposite."

Susan gave a laugh. "Good advice is too often comprised of telling others your opinion of what is best for them."

"Yes, it is. However, you need not heed a word

of it."

"Is this where you now tell me to follow my heart?" Susan smoothed the blue ribbons that fell down the front of her white, sprig muslin dress.

"Oh, no, never that. The heart is quite as unreliable as the head. Your mind will rationalize almost anything, and the heart—well, it often wants things for no better a reason than to want them. I would recommend you make your choices on one simple thought—does this make me happy?"

Stopping, Susan turned her stare onto Davinia. She dropped her arm from Davinia's and began to pleat one of the ribbons, a frown pulling her eyebrows flat. "You sound as if your choices left you unhappy."

Davinia shook her head, and resisted glancing over at Everley. She took Susan's gloved hands in hers. "Life has a habit of introducing enough unhappy times without any effort on our part. Besides, these are your choices we speak of. Mine have—"

"Do not tell me you are ancient and are past making choices." Susan squeezed Davinia's fingers. "You speak as if you are some ancient crone, when in fact there is not even a dozen years between our ages."

"Yes, but there is an age of experience in the world, and my experiences have led me to believe that while it may seem mortifying to say that one has made a mistake, it is better to say such a thing while matters can still be changed. Just remember that—and remember to keep asking what it is that makes you happy."

Frowning hard now, Susan pulled her hands away. "Does this have to do with your argument with Everley?"

Davinia almost let out a growl of frustration. She blew out a breath and asked, "How do you know of that?"

"Everyone in the household knows. The duke's valet told Father's valet who told the housekeeper who told Mother's maid who confided in my maid. And you have not answered."

"This has to do with your future, Susan, and your having told your mother you intend to have Lord Leifmere... eventually. I hope that is not an understanding set in stone. Now, if you will excuse me, I—" Davinia stalled on finding an excuse as to why she needed to put distance between herself and her niece. This had nothing to do with the duke or her argument with him, she told herself. Except the uncomfortable slide of a tingle over her skin left her fearing her niece was poking a very sore spot of guilt and... and something else she did not want to look into.

Thankfully, Susan spared her any need for words. She smiled, said she must go see what valentine card Miss Mosby had been given, and took herself off. Davinia took up the fan that had been hanging from her elbow and plied it. She needed air—lots of it. Since it was freezing outside, she headed for the door, slipped out, and made for Freddy's study.

Chapter Twelve

"I begin to believe this is your bolt hole, not your brother's." Everley shut the door to Somerton's study behind him. He had already cursed himself as a fool for watching Davinia. He had promised himself he would keep a respectable distance and that he would ignore her the best he could. Instead, he'd seen her slip from the drawing room, her color high on her cheeks, her breathing fast and shallow, and her steps quick. He had told himself whatever set-to she'd had with her niece was nothing to him. She must have picked another quarrel. That was Davinia. His good intentions lasted all of a minute, and then he followed her from the drawing room, catching a glimpse of her reddish gown as the door to Somerton's study clicked shut.

Davinia had been pacing in front of an unlit fire. She stopped now to face him. Everley thought at first to summon a servant to light the fire, changed his mind and strode to the hearth. A tinderbox sat on the mantle. He took it up, bent low, struck flint to steel, and sparked an ember that grew fast to a flame. Good dry wood and duff caught at once—the staff knew how to set a fire. Straightening, he found Davinia watching him, arms folded over her chest, her shawl clutched tight. A lamp had been lit on the desk and gave off a yellow glow that did not quite reach the corners of the room.

Everley gestured to one of the wing chairs. "No chess, I promise you. But please sit so that I may as well. My ankle is advising me I have been on my feet far too long."

She did not smile. However, she did sit down. "I wouldn't have thought you cared to try your luck again in Freddy's study. Things did not go so well when...oh, blast and bother, it was my fault. I beg your pardon. However, I shall no doubt be equally aggravating shortly. I have been informed I have a sad lack of tact due to my unfortunate upbringing."

Sweeping his coat tails aside, Everley sank into the high-backed chair opposite. He suppressed the urge to give a sigh of relief and leaned back. "No wonder you took yourself off, your color high."

"One thing explained but not why you followed me. Are more lectures due? I promise to try and endure them, but what with my temper being uncertain, we may end at loggerheads again."

He held up a hand. Firelight glinted from his signet ring. Wood smoke had begun to weave a pleasant aroma into the room along with heat. "I have not come to reform your character, nor to criticize."

"You're here for the brandy?"

He shook his head. "That did not go so well earlier, either. I should—"

"No." She fluttered her hands and then folded them into her lap. "No more shoulds. I am done with them, along with oughts and musts and obligations that simply dig a hole for me."

"You dislike expectations?"

"Do they not lead mostly to disappointments? My mother expected me to behave better. My father expected me to have some sort of artistic flair—of which I have none. My brother expects I shall live with him until my dying day, and is that not a depressing thought?"

"Dying days generally are, but why such gloom?"

She glanced down at her hands. Everley noted she had clenched them tight, but now she unfolded her fists and smoothed her gloves. She pressed her fingers down against her thighs. He could see the outline of her legs clearly with her skirt pressed close and couldn't help but notice a pleasing, soft curve. Dragging his eyes back to her face, he crossed his legs and wondered what the devil he was doing here, sitting by a fireside with Davinia when he ought to be attending his host's ball. But he knew. They'd once been friends, he and Davinia, before that debacle in the garden.

For a moment, she said nothing. The wood crackled in the fire and shadows danced over her face. She looked tired, he thought. A little drawn now the color had fled her face. Fine lines could be seen around her mouth from where she smiled too often. Everley realized he had no such marks on his face, despite the fact that he had more years on him than Davinia.

Looking up at last, she said, "I had been advising my niece to think more on what will make her happy and make her choices accordingly, and I realized I have never taken my own advice. It is a lowering thought."

Uncrossing his legs, he leaned forward. "You are unhappy here?"

She looked at the fire, seeing into the flames—or perhaps seeing into another time. "No, not unhappy. However, I cannot claim happiness, either. I am content, but—" Breaking off, she gave him a level stare. "Tonight I had a glimpse ahead, to my going to London with Susan, watching after her, seeing her into starting her own life, and then...then what have I to do? Sit with Felicity and embroider slippers with flowers that look like giraffes? Manage Freddy's estate books for him? Take up some hobby that is a ladylike bore? I am too much like a loose thread here."

"So marry again." The words cost him much to say. He disliked the notion that she could—she would—marry another man. He did not care to look too deeply at the unease the thought cost him, but he shifted in his chair and put his stare on the slowly dying flames. He ought to put another log on the fire. "You are young enough. From what I've heard, you won't come to the match without money. You have connections."

She gave a small laugh, and he glanced back at her to see if her amusement was real or if she intended irony. Her mouth curved, and she shook her head. Her hair, pulled up and back into some sort of braid, was slowly coming undone, and wisps curled around her face and her bright eyes. "I am not that young, have never been that pretty, the funds I bring with me are not that huge, and this war with France goes on and on, leaving an imbalance of far too many ladies seeking husbands and far too few young gentlemen looking for wives. Perhaps I should be a second or third pick for some fellow looking at a second or third wife, a fellow who would not mind being a second husband. He might even have a household of children, and I could become a nagging stepmother to them."

"I do not think that would make you happy."

Her mouth twisted down on one side. "And we are back to my original premise. I have not taken my own advice. I very much fear it is because I am not quite certain what will make me happy."

The thought popped into his head that he could—he had—made her happy. She'd been happy the day he'd kissed her. She'd always been happy to argue with him, to take him down a peg or two. She'd been happy to discuss books or politics or even the ridiculous eccentricities of fashion they had glimpsed in Hyde Park during the hour or two when society went on parade. She'd ridden with him in his curricle, always urging him to set a smarter pace, teasing him that he should allow her to take the reins for a turn so she could show him her driving skills. He had never done that. He wondered now what else he had missed out on.

Uncomfortable with the direction this conversation was taking, he rose, limped to the fire, took up the poker, and stirred the logs, thrusting at them until the fire leapt up again. He became aware of Davinia at his side. She took the poker from him, her gloved hand brushing over his with a touch of warmth. "You will set the house on fire if you keep jabbing at that log as if it is a dragon you intend to slay."

He turned toward her. She smelled of pungent wood smoke and a sweet hint of lavender. She stood close enough that he could put his arm about her. He did not, however. Her upper arm brushed his, and she glanced up at him, lips parted, eyes suddenly wide as if she had realized how close she stood to him.

He opened his mouth to say something, but he was uncertain again of the words that ought to come out. It was too much like that time in the garden, when he had kissed her and ought to have said something, but now he knew why his words stalled, and it was not due to the notion that Wycliffe men married at thirty. He could say he admired her, that he cared for her, that he wished to make her happy—and she would give that luscious laugh of hers. She would tell him not to be a tease and turn away, and she would have the right of it.

She would mock him, and rightly so, for their

expectations in life were at odds. Expectations—she had the right of it there. They led to disappointment.

She turned away to put the poker back into the set of fire tools and kept her eyes down as she moved. With the poker safely stowed, she tugged up her gloves as if they had slipped out of place. "I must get back. Felicity will be missing me, and I must see if she managed to get Mercer to thin the punch. Please do not feel obliged to return to the festivities. I am more than happy to make your apologies to Freddy and Felicity, for you have the excuse of your injuries to give you a reason to escape." At the door, she paused and glanced back. Her words had come out in a rush, but now her voice dropped to almost a whisper. "Thank you for coming after me. It was kind." With a smile, she slipped out of the room, taking with her that hint of lavender and that unsettling energy she brought with her.

Everley turned to stare into the fire.

It had not been kindness that had prompted him to follow her. Madness, yes. Those ridiculous impulses, left to him by that unsteady ancestor whose blood flowed in him, had been at fault, too. But mostly it had been a realization that he did not like to see Davinia without her usual glint of mischief in her eyes and that beguiling smile.

Which left him thinking over her words about making choices for happiness, and how that seemed impossible for anyone burdened with the duties that came with a venerable title, a firm drilling of obligations, and the expectations put upon him by an ancient family name.

Chapter Thirteen

Everley was departing Somerton today. Davinia stood at the window, watching the drive, wondering why she had put herself here in the breakfast room where she might get a last glimpse of his back as he left. She had a cold cup of tea in her hands, fractured toast left behind on her plate on the breakfast table, and a hollow feeling inside that she put down to an uneasy rest the previous night. She lifted her chin. She could be proud of herself—yes, proud. Over the past ten days, she and Everley had bumped along without so much as a cross word. She'd put on her best manners, despite the temptation Everley had thrown her way when he pushed that bad leg of his too hard. She had even resisted teasing him. Now, he was taking his leave, and she told herself it was all for the best.

Of course the man had to turn and glance in her direction.

She stepped back, away from the window, her fingers clutching the china, one hand lifted to touch the locket she wore. With the sun behind his back—pale and struggling to provide some sort of warmth this late in February—he must not be able to see her. But that glance—so certain and abrupt—unsettled her. She pushed out a breath.

Oh, just go.

But now he was bowing to Felicity and shaking Freddy's hand. Susan had also come down to say her goodbyes and dropped a very pretty curtsy to the duke. Davinia let out a breath and gulped down her cold tea. Well, she could at least rest easy on one point—Susan would not marry the duke, but Everley was off back to London to find himself a bride and would no doubt have some other well-bred young lady with a huge dowry fixed to his side in no time at all. Frowning, Davinia decided it must be the weather giving her the blue-devils, what with a cold wind blowing from the north and a clear sky and hard, dry roads.

Turning from the scene, she told herself not to listen for the rumble of the carriage wheels taking Everley away, nor to note the harness jingling, but she did look up as Freddy and Felicity stepped into the breakfast room. Susan followed, chattering on about when the family would depart for London as well.

"Early April is a good time for London." Susan plopped down in a chair. "Or March. That would give time to order the dresses I shall need for the season."

Felicity swept into a chair and poured tea. "Susan, please do not slouch. That is a dreadful habit you have from your father. If you are in such a hurry to depart, you had best sort out what you will pack and bring with you. Your riding habit is perfectly in fashion, and you have several new dresses that need only trim to refresh them. Your father will see you well attired, but do not expect him to drain the estate for this or any other season. Is that not the gist of it, my lord?" She turned to Freddy.

When Freddy failed to answer, Davinia glanced at him and found him staring at her, a line tight between his eyebrows. She squirmed in her chair. "Coffee, Freddy? Or shall I order you a mug of ale?"

"Why are you here?" The question came out as if blurted without a thought.

Blinking, Davinia swapped a glance with Felicity, who was now also frowning. Susan sat up, eyes bright.

After wetting her lips, Davinia said, "Well, I had thought to partake of breakfast, Freddy. Or do you mean that as a more general question, such as why am I here and not also packing for London?"

"I mean, why are you here and not with Everley. Why are you letting the dashed man gallop off again?"

Davinia forced a laugh. "I do not think Everley gallops anywhere and certainly not when he's had a doctor's warning to have a care for his ribs."

"That's not what I mean, and you know it." Freddy waved a vague hand. "Here you are, letting the fellow get away from you again, and now you'll mope about—"

"I never moped!"

"Oh, you did. I had letter after letter from Mother the last time you allowed Everley to slip from your grasp."

Davinia put down her cup with a sharp rap. "Freddy, the man is not a fish I must land." Susan giggled, and Davinia shot the girl a narrow-eyed glance. Susan dropped her stare to her lap and begged pardon in a quiet voice. Turning back to her brother, Davinia fought for what she hoped might be a superior and calming tone. "You make too much of this."

"I do not." Freddy crossed his arms over his chest and spread his booted feet wide. Davinia let out a breath. This promised to be more of a brangle than she had ever expected, and now she wished she had remained in her room. "Mother wanted me to call the fellow out last time."

Stiffening, Davinia stared at her brother, her mouth falling open. She snapped it closed, swallowed, and then said, "Nonsense."

"That's dashed well what I wrote back to Mother

at the time. Calling a duke out! And for what—a kiss he'd given you in a garden."

Now Felicity and Susan both gasped. Davinia fought not to look at either of them. This was between herself and Freddy. She stood, pushing back the chair from the table with a scrape of the legs on the floor. "I will not have this conversation with you about ancient history."

"Oh ho, I only wish it were ancient. Don't you think I've seen the two of you, dancing about each other? You've strong feelings for the fellow, but you're too stubborn to admit it, and...you're afraid. I always knew you'd cry craven if you ever met the fellow again. Just like you did in that garden."

"How do you—?" Davinia broke off the question. "Mother!"

"Yes, mother. She wrote pages and pages about you and 'the garden incident.' Took me nearly a week to decipher the whole of it, but I have to say, I thought you had more backbone. Now, here you are again. Ready to descend into the sulks because—"

"Will you stop saying that! I do not sulk or mope!"

"You'll do both, and you'll be dragging about again all because you won't face the fact that you care about the fellow, and you're not certain he returns your regard. You're afraid to try and bring him up to snuff. Afraid you'll fall short."

Felicity spilled her tea. "Lord Somerton! Are you urging your sister to entertain becoming the duke's—" She broke off, glanced at Susan, and then dropped her voice low. "His *chaufferette?*"

Davinia frowned at Felicity. "I am no one's bed-warmer, and of course Susan knows exactly what you reference. She did have a most excellent governess who taught her French."

Cheeks pink, Felicity huffed out a breath and busied herself pouring more tea. "This is not a conversation I wish to have at the breakfast table. Susan, you may retire."

"But, Mama, I haven't eaten." Susan stood and immediately filled a plate. Sitting down, she pushed a large slice of bacon into her mouth and glared back at her mother.

Davinia could see this conversation was headed nowhere good and turned back to Freddy. "You are upsetting your wife."

"Ha!" Freddy dropped his arms to his side. "Upsetting you more like, with a few home truths. Dash it, Davie, I don't want to see you unhappy. Go after Everley. Kiss the damn fellow and see if he don't kiss you back, and make certain the fellow proposes this time 'round or, duke or not, I shall call the dashed fellow out afterwards."

"My lord, your language. And please do consider, Davinia is beyond wonderful, but we all are fully aware she would make a terrible duchess."

Freddy glanced at his wife, eyebrows lifting high. Davinia considered the possibility that she ought to tell them both to go jump into the nearest river. Her brother interrupted before she could. "It's not about being a bad duchess, it's about making Everley a decent wife. The fellow's headed to becoming a stick if he's not careful."

"I said the same thing." Susan waved her fork in a small circle.

Turning her stare on her niece, Davinia lifted a warning finger. "You may stay out of this, miss."

Tucking his thumbs into his waistcoat pockets, Freddy rocked back on his heels. "I dare you to go after Everley."

"Somerton," Felicity said, a warning in her voice.

Face hot, Davinia stepped forward until she stood toe-to-toe with her brother. "Dare? You dare me? I am not some child who can be taunted into misbehaving."

"A coward. That's what you are. You were then, you are now. The man embarrassed you, or at least his family did. It smarted, and you expect the same'll happen again. Well, I'll lay a monkey it won't." Unhooking a thumb, he stuck out his hand. "Well, Davie? Are you going to back down—again?"

He said it with such a sneer in his voice that Davinia's blood heated. She fisted her hands in her skirt. She would not allow him to taunt her. But a knowing look had entered his eyes. Freddy gave a smug nod and started to turn away.

Pushing past him, she strode for the door. "You will owe me five hundred pounds when I return."

***

Everley had thought to drive on through Mersey—the village really held no attraction for him given its association with his recent carriage accident. However, he had not calculated on the plague of his injuries. The rocking of the carriage and the jarring from hitting what seemed to be every pothole in the road had him more than ready to call a temporary halt to his journey. He thought to fortify himself with a good porter from the inn and to perhaps vent some of his ill temper on 'Old Tom.' He was balked of the second option by the fact that the landlord had made himself scarce on some errand or other. Everley settled himself in the public room with a clay mug and a rather good porter. He also began to think he should change his direction for Kettlewell Hall. His estate lay only a few miles to the south, and just now that seemed an inordinately attractive distance. The doctor had had the right of it with his advice to allow more time for bones to knit. Why not stop at Kettlewell Hall? While he had sent Bishops and his luggage onward to London in another coach, his staff at Kettlewell Hall would have made all ready for a visit. It had indeed been too long since he'd last been to see that estate, and he could always send word to Bishops to turn around.

With his decision made, Everley decided to finish his porter and alter his course. He would have no need to change horses, he would have a comfortable bed in a short time, and he would have no distracting Davinia to ignore. Such a decision, he told himself, had nothing to do with keeping himself anywhere near her vicinity.

He took his time with his drink. It did little to take the pain from his ankle, but at least his sore ribs had returned to being nothing more than an inconvenience. After laying down two shillings on the scarred oak bar, for his drink and the trouble of fetching it for him, he stepped outside. Clouds scudded across the sky, thick and warning of more rain, and bare tree branches shivered in an east wind. Everley started to pull on his gloves. A flash of red drew his gaze to the fields where a few sheep grazed on winter grass. A giant of a chestnut horse cleared a stone fence across the far field, disappeared behind a hedge, and then reappeared on the nearby road. Everley muttered a curse under his breath. That, if he did not mistake matters, was Somerton's rawboned hunter—the wide, white blaze on the horse's face was easy to remark. Drumming his fingers against his thigh, he waited.

In another few moments, Davinia trotted smartly down the road on Somerton's hunter. The horse held his head high, and his breath misted in puffs before him. Davinia drew rein in front of the Brown Boar, her color high, her riding habit mud spattered and her hat askew. Both she and the horse seemed to be breathing hard.

Everley had to look up at her. He lifted an eyebrow. "Is it your intent to break your neck? That field is little more than a bog, and it is a wonder your brother's horse did not pull a tendon."

She slipped her foot out from the stirrup and slid from the saddle. The horse rubbed his sweaty head against her side and then sidled a few steps, obviously still ready to run.

"You need to walk him," Everley noted. He lifted a hand to summon a groom to take the sweating horse. Davinia relinquished the reins without comment, her color still high, and worry slid across Everley's skin. "Is something wrong? At Somerton?"

She shook her head and bit down on her lower lip. "I—I..." Twisting her riding crop between gloved hands, she stammered, "I forgot to say good-bye."

He had to blink at that. "Forgot? You gallop as if the hounds of hell are on your heels, and that is why?"

Clutching her riding crop even tighter, she nodded, and then admitted, "Well, actually Freddy dared me. He..." She let the words fade and stepped forward.

Everley stepped back. "What in all the heavens is wrong?"

She let out a long breath. "Oh, I can't do this here, in the middle of the village green of all places.

Please tell me you bespoke a private parlor within?"

"I have not, but I easily can." He waved for her to precede him into the inn. The commotion of the galloping horse had drawn some attention from the few souls on the street and those within the public room—mostly old men in tattered clothes that spoke of a lack of profession. Everley ushered Davinia onwards, managed to get them into a parlor at the back, ordered hot tea, and had the landlady, who seemed to want to linger, sent on her way. Wondering what disaster had occurred now, he turned to face Davinia.

She was still fretting her riding crop. Everley pulled off his hat and gloves, tossed them onto a nearby table. He left his greatcoat on. The room was not large, but the smoldering fire in the grate did little to warm it. With a table, two straight-backed chairs, a couch whose floral upholstery had seen better days, faded wallpaper, and limp curtains, the room could not be said to provide many comforts. The place smelled of ale, tobacco, and a touch of damp mold.

Before he could again ask Davinia what troubled her, a knock on the door interrupted. Mrs. Trotter, the landlady, and a dark-haired maid swept in with tea on a tray, cakes, and apologies for the struggling fire. Mrs. Trotter, a thin woman with graying hair pulled severely back, had the maid settle the tray upon the table and stoke the fire with fresh coal. She offered to take Everley's greatcoat and Davinia's gloves and made a general nuisance of herself. Digging out the purse from his greatcoat pocket, Everley managed to get the landlady and her maid from the room with the bribe of a few coins. Finally, he had the door shut on her.

Turning back to Davinia, he wondered what the devil could be amiss. He could not believe she had galloped a good twelve miles for no better reason than to wish him Godspeed.

She stood facing him, her hands gripped tight, the mud splatters drying on her riding habit—something in a military style in a dark green. He had the urge to pull out a handkerchief and wipe the splatters from her face, but he was not quite certain the gesture would be appreciated. He at least pulled out the linen from his pocket and tossed it onto the table. "You're muddy."

She let out a sharp laugh, but she took up his handkerchief. "Muddled more like. I...drat, I rehearsed what I should say a dozen times on the way here. I also almost pulled up, but Arthur took the bit in his teeth at the second field. He's been too long in his stall, and you would have thought him a green colt, not a staid old gentleman."

"Davinia—?"

"Yes, yes, I know I am babbling." She put a hand to her face and brushed at another splatter of mud. "It's a wonder Arthur settled to a trot in Mersey, but he was blown by then. And I...well, I have a confession to make."

Everley stiffened as if she had struck him. He held up a hand. "Please. I've rather had my fill of confidences of late. You've more than made clear your feelings when it comes to me. Will you take some tea?"

She twisted her gloved fingers together. "No, that is exactly what I have not done. I mean about the confidences, not the tea. At least according to Freddy. I have avoided and not clarified and been rather, well, more than rather spiteful because of old hurts. But tea sounds perfectly lovely." She moved to the table where the teapot and cups rested upon a lacquered tray and splashed the pale brown liquid into the cups, spilling more than she poured. Swearing under her breath, she clattered the china pot back onto the tray. "Oh, this is useless, as am I, and I knew I should be."

Retreating back across the room, Everley dragged off his greatcoat and threw it over the back of a chair. The room had become intolerably warm. "I begin to have the feeling that not even tea will salvage this situation. Davinia, what has you acting as if you have lost your senses?"

"That! That is exactly the problem. I have lost them. Lost them ages ago. Never recovered. Oh, I thought I had. I thought I'd recovered, but Freddy is right. I never quite did. And now I am making a mull of this again. I knew I should, which is why I never wanted…I—oh, drat it!" She came around the table and stopped in front of him. "If I am going to mortify myself yet again, I might as well do it up utterly." Reaching up, she put a hand on his shoulder, pulled him down to her, and pressed her lips to his.

The move stunned him. For a moment, he could only stand there, stiff and cold and wondering if Davinia had indeed become moonstruck. Her lips pressed against his, hard yet warm—he would almost say inviting—and her scent wound around him, stealing away his thoughts, leaving him light-headed.

Letting go of him, she stepped back and gave a firm nod. "There. It's done. I should have done that years ago. Except I could not have done that on Oxford Street, and that garden was already an utter travesty of anything social." Reaching up, she undid the top button to her riding habit and started to fuss with something at her neck.

Everley frowned. "Really now, I must ask your

intentions here. Do you mean to disrobe? To somehow—?"

"Oh, stop talking as if I wanted to compromise myself with you. Here!" She unfastened a necklace and held out the gold chain and locket.

Wary, he stepped closer. She pushed the locket at him again. He took it and cracked it open. A small pale-blue flower had been pressed flat and tucked into the frame. Everley frowned at it for a moment. A bluebell?

Davinia put up her chin. "You probably do not recall, but I meant to tuck it into your waistcoat that day, only I never did."

He looked up at her, his chest hollow and his mind spinning. "You kept it? All this time? I do remember. What is it? A reminder of your folly?"

"A reminder of you." She touched a finger to the back of his hand. "I shan't trouble you again. I've already been informed what a terrible duchess I should make, and…and there's not much else we could be to each other, and you'll be glad to see the back of me, I am certain."

"Who told you such a thing?" He waved the locket at her. "About being a terrible duchess?" She would, of course, be just that. However, the image suddenly flashed into his mind of her descending the stairs at his home seat in Surrey, a smile on her face and mischief in her eyes. He rubbed a hand over his eyes and then stared at her again.

Davinia lifted one shoulder in a shrug. "Felicity said so and with good cause. She has the right of it. However, Susan also said perhaps I could help you avoid becoming such a stick—"

"Stick!"

"Ah, see—Susan has the right of it, too, for you

would not poker up if it were not true. You would laugh. But I wanted you to know that I did care for you—a great deal. And...and, well, Freddy dared me."

He stiffened. "This is a dare then? A jest? Dash it, Davinia, you're muddling me now. I cannot tell what you mean in earnest and what is some sort of jape."

Fluttering her hands, she said, "It is no jest. Not this part. I ought to have spoken up in that dratted garden oh so long ago, but I was beyond mortified then. I didn't want to find out that...well, that all you meant to give me was a slip on the shoulder."

"Davinia, really? That's what you thought of me?"

"Well, did you intend a proposal, what with your father glaring and my mother tearing into you? Yes, a fine romantic moment, and I never should have known if you cared or had simply had your hand forced. No, it would not do!" Color flared on her cheeks. Her lower lip trembled. She pulled in a breath and seemed to force the words out. "I love you, Everley. I probably always will. You are maddening and too starched for your own good, and well, perhaps I ought to have pressed you to marry me back then. However, I would have come between you and your family. Or you would have come between me and mine, and that wasn't something that suited either of us. You have been quite right about all of that. But...be happy, will you please? Marry Susan if you wish, or anyone else you care to, but do marry to make yourself happy and not just to suit some notion settled upon you by the expectations of others. They really don't matter as much as you think—I have learned that much. And...and well, I wish that much for you." She turned and fled from the room, leaving Everley looking at the locket and the faded bluebell.

Frowning, he stared after Davinia. She was doing

it again—running from him. She was wise to do so. He could not possibly marry her. She was too opinionated, too headstrong, too...well, too Davinia. She would upset his world. She would...

Oh, hell.

Breaking off the thought, he started after her. Dash it, but she was not running out on him. Not again. Besides, she had left her gloves and her riding crop—and that dashed locket in his hand. He gathered up her things and strode for the door, stopping only for a brief word with the landlady as to the stabling of Davinia's horse and his own team.

He found Davinia outside the inn, standing with her arms crossed, glancing up and down the lane as if expecting something. "I asked them to care for your mount," he told her.

She swung around. "Of course you would. Well, I shall have them saddle another horse, then."

"No, you won't." It had started to rain. The world smelled of damp grass, of horse from Davinia's skirts, and the faint hint of lavender that Davinia brought with her. Mist settled on her upturned face, wilting the feather curling around her hat. The damp chilled his shoulders. "You started this." He held out the locket. "You kept the flower."

She glanced down at it and waved a bare, pale hand. "Yes. Foolishly sentimental of me, but there it is."

Closing his fist around the locket, he stepped closer to her so she had to look up at him. "It never occurred to me until just now why I left thoughts of marriage so late."

"You were waiting to turn thirty." She wrinkled her nose. "A fine age to marry. You told me so yourself and no doubt had your father tell that same thing to you numerous times."

"Yes, but I might have chosen a wife long before now and settled for a long engagement. I searched for someone, you know, and yes, I made lists. Unsatisfactory lists, for I could not find your smile again. No one had your laugh, Davinia. No one tormented me as you did. No one made me smile, or brightened a room, and I could not keep any of their names in my head. But you—I never forgot you, Davinia, and not because you were the only one to turn me away. No, it was your scent, your maddening ways, and the fact that well…I always felt a person with you Davinia, and not so much simply a duke's heir. Do you know how many times I went over and over what I would say to you if we ever met again?" He started to take her hand, found he had her riding crop and gloves in his grip. He tucked them under his arm and took her hands in his. "I don't know what I meant that day in the garden when I kissed you. But I do know it was the only time I acted on impulse and did what I wished." He shook his head. "No, strike that. I acted once before, when I was a boy of eight and stole from the house with my fishing rod, slipping from my tutor's grasp on a day too fine to stay indoors. My father caned me hard for that, and I took the lesson to heart not to act on what I wished. I had expectations to meet, and I've done so. Or at least I did so until that day in the garden. You pushed at me until I gave into my worse instincts—or so I thought. Now I am uncertain if they are not my better ones."

She had been staring at her hands, held tight in his grip. Now she looked up at him, her eyes wide and wary. "And how do you find out which is the case?"

"I could kiss you again. Properly. That peck you

just gave me proved unsatisfactory due to its brevity and too much trepidation."

She stepped closer. "Trepidation? Well, of course there was. I shall have you know a lady is not supposed to go around kissing gentlemen, not even if she is a widow and—"

Dropping her riding crop and her gloves to the mud, he put his arms around her and pulled her close. "And what?"

"Oh, hush and kiss me. Kiss me and then let me go, Everley, for you know things will never work out between us."

"How do I know that? Will you make me a terrible duchess? Or will you—as you said Susan put it—keep me from becoming a stick?"

"She ought not to have said that, but Freddy said the same, and I really ought not to have repeated anything of that to you."

"Yes, but you think it is true—all because I did not laugh at the idea."

"What of all those expectations upon you? Your title, your position, your—?"

"Oh, hang the lot of them. For once at least. I've gone mad, and I find I rather like the sensation, or perhaps that is the sensation of you in my arms. You fit to me, Davinia. You always have, and I should be a fool not to recognize that much. Besides, you said yourself I should marry to make myself happy. Would you do that? Make me happy?"

"No. I shall argue with you and try to bring you down a peg whenever you become 'the duke.' I shall not add to your consequences in the least. I am not so young you can mold me to meet your requirements, and the rest of your family—whom I am given to understand is numerous—will no doubt despise me for having that faint touch of trade in my family."

A smile tugged at him. "Well, that is a good reason right there for our being happy. Fewer relatives around is a positive note that quite tips the argument in your favor. I think I must kiss you, and then you shall have to marry me."

"You think I would be compromised? That I will expect marriage all because of a kiss? Impossible. I didn't before, and as I have said, I'm a widow, and besides that I never had much of a reputation to lose."

"Yes, but I am a duke of upstanding virtue, and you will compromise me greatly if you do not marry me after I kiss you here in a public thoroughfare. It is my expectations you must now consider, or at least I would have you do so, for I will not have you giving me the reputation of a rake, a care-for-nobody who—"

"Oh, hush up and kiss me if you are going to do so."

He bent over her, fit his lips to hers, and proceeded to take his time with this kiss. She parted her lips when he teased her with a flick of his tongue, and then he was lost to anything but the feel of her. She had him dizzy with need. She stole his breath and his mind, and years fell away as if they had never existed. He would swear he was back in that garden in London, Davinia soft and yielding in his arms, delightfully so.

A cold drop of rain down the back of his neck brought him back to his senses. A catcall whistle and clapping had him pulling away from Davinia to glare at two grooms, a grinning maid, and an elderly couple who averted their eyes and hurried past.

Davinia let out a sigh. "Oh, bother, that is the Fletchers, and the missus is the biggest gossip in

Mersey."

Everley released Davinia, bent to retrieve her crop and gloves, and then offered his arm. "Come inside. It is cold, I am getting wet—as are you—and we have settled nothing."

She put a hand on his sleeve and followed him back into the private parlor. The tea had gone cold, but Everley ordered the makings of a hot punch and closed the door firmly on the gawking maid. Davinia stood in front of the fire, rubbing her arms. She pulled off her wet hat and tossed it onto the horrible flowered sofa and turned to him. "Do you really think we could make a match of it? I shall be nothing but a headache for you—I know I shall."

"Yes, you will no doubt continue to be a disaster. However, you make me smile. You poke at my consequences, and you may indeed keep me from becoming a stick. I once thought of you as much like a comet, but I actually think you are more a ray of sunshine on a gloomy day. Davinia, I have no idea if love conquers all, but I do know I have thought too often of you—and seeing you again...well, blast it, I don't want to let you go. I did so once, and I told myself it was for the best and something you wanted as well. Finding out that is not the case makes a huge difference. I want to do what I want for once and tell the world to go to perdition. Perhaps it is the blood of my dashed loose screw of an ancestor rising up to overwhelm every bit of my training, but by all accounts he had a long and happy marriage, and he married to please himself."

"How utterly shocking of him." Rubbing her arms, Davinia smiled.

He came to her side and started to rub her arms

for her. A knock interrupted before he could do more. He swore softly, but the landlady and maid bustled in and settled to making hot punch beside the fire. Davinia edged closer to him. "There are times when being a duke has its advantages. I never should have got such prompt service."

Everley pulled out more coins and ordered the landlady and the maid from the room, saying he at least knew how to make his own punch. They left, the landlady craning through the door crack for one last look as Everley shut it upon her.

Davinia laughed. "Well, now I have truly compromised you, for it shall be all over Mersey within the hour that I've kissed you and had you in a private parlor to myself. But are you really certain about this, Everley?"

"Not in the least. But if you don't have me, I shall end up married to no one, for the last names on my list are ones I shall cross off. It's you or no one, Davinia. I have come to that firm realization. So will you have me and save me from my dreadful fate of a solitary life with nothing but relatives to make me unhappy? Will you please marry me and make me a perfectly awful duchess who will do nothing to live up to expectations but who will do everything to make me smile at times, and who is indeed the one choice of my heart?"

Epilogue

Davinia stared at the list of names. She nibbled on one knuckle and twirled the quill she had just sharpened. Outside the study window, birds twittered, sunshine warmed the air with a touch of true spring and not another rainy day. Inside, with invitations fresh from the printers, stacked and awaiting addressing, the study did not seem half as inviting. Bother, but was she really expected to ask half the world and its brother to attend?

Fortunately, Dudley interrupted, coming in with the morning post. She looked up at him and asked, "Must I really invite all these…?" She waved a hand at the list, which seemed to go on for pages.

Dudley deposited the post in its usual spot on the corner of the mahogany desk, came around to her side, and adjusted his spectacles. "The ballroom here at Everley House holds no more than five hundred. A hundred may be comfortably seated for dinner. I would advise being selective to ensure any invitation from the Duchess of Everley retains a certain cachet."

Rubbing a spot between her eyebrows, Davinia tried to will a headache to form—anything to remove her from this obligation she had undertaken. "A hundred. Oh, lud—what if it is the wrong hundred?" She threw down the quill and glanced up at Dudley. "Why oh why did I ever think I could be a duchess to Everley? I shall disgrace him. I shall bring disaster down upon this wretched ball, and all because—" She choked off the words.

Dudley pulled off his spectacles and put a hand on her shoulder. "I shall give you the advice my father gave me upon taking up a position in a duke's household. Take deep breaths and concentrate not upon the expectations of others but on what you can and are able to do."

"Did he really say all that?"

He removed his hand from her shoulder and pulled out a handkerchief to clean his spectacles. "What he actually said was 'buck up, you'll do,' but I put my own interpretation upon his words. My father is not a man given to many words. However, he means well."

"As do I, but intent and action are so often too far apart in this world." She waved a hand at the invitations and the list. "I fear I will fall very short as a duchess, and Everley will grow tired of my failures, and there is nothing he can do about it now we are married, other than send me to the country to rusticate."

"Your grace, if you will allow me the observation, you have already done better than most duchesses. You have a happy husband, something I never expected to see in the Duke of Everley. You must be aware there are duchesses who reside only in the countryside, refusing to come to town with their husbands, who lavish more affection on the dogs they breed than on anything else. Yet other duchesses have been known to bring their families near to bankruptcy with fatal gambling habits. We shall not go into the list of duchesses in past decades whose scheming meant heads severed for treason to the crown. Please do not think a title elevates the mind or the soul. It brings obligations to those willing to undertake them, riches if one has sense enough not to squander them—which narrows the field considerably—and a useful status if one has the will to put it to use. A duchess, if she is kind-hearted and good-natured, may help lighten the load of all that. The duke may not smile often—he is not a gentleman given to smiles—but I see in him a lightness I never thought to exist. That is your doing, your grace."

Davinia put a hand to her chest. Tears stung her eyes. "Do you really think so?"

Before Dudley could answer, the door clicked open, and Everley strode in. "Dudley, are you flirting with my wife or making her cry? If it is the former, I shall have to let you go, and that would be deuced inconvenient for you are an excellent secretary. If it is the latter, there is nothing for it but to call you out, and if I have to flee the country due to having murdered you in an illegal duel, I shall be cross with you."

Dudley fitted his spectacles back in place. "Rest assured, it is neither, your grace. I am here merely to offer advice and assistance with planning the ball."

"Ball?" Everley stopped in front of his desk and faced Davinia. "What ball? Why are we hosting a ball?"

Sitting upright and brushing at her eyes, Davinia said, "For Susan. She's making her bow at court shortly, and I've offered to host a ball for her. I meant it to be the event of the season, but it seems more likely to turn into the debacle of the decade." She waved a hand at the invitations and the list.

Everley came around the desk, taking Dudley's place beside her. He picked up her list. "Where did you come by this?"

"Your Aunt Earnesta gave the names to me. She called to take tea the other day, and when I mentioned the ball, she said she might help for she knows most of the right people and all your relations."

"Good God, she's got Great-Uncle Sylvester on here—he's been dead for twenty years. And the Russels? No, that won't do, you cannot invite both brothers. They swore an oath to kill each other on next sighting, but they're well into their sixties now and would be put out to have to carry out that vow. As to Aunt Octavia, she's ninety and in mourning for her favorite son, who died last year at seventy-two. She would be insulted to be forced between putting off her blacks to attend or turning you down, and she'd never forgive you." He threw the list down upon the desk. "Earnesta is up to her tricks. She's the sort who would snip the traces just to see if your horses might bolt free when someone cracked the whip and then act surprised when they did."

Davinia frowned. "She seemed quite nice when she called. We had a long chat."

"Oh, she is polite enough, but she nurtures strongly held revolutionary beliefs. She thinks the entire family ought to throw in with the ideals of freedom, liberty, and equality, renounce our titles, behead the king, and burn down most of London. She actually made a trip to France when their revolution began and got sent back here. I suspect she was too radical even for the French."

Davinia gave a dry laugh. "Well, bother. She must be out to bring down society with disastrous balls."

Everley took up her hand. "Stop fretting. If Lady Somerton can pull off a Valentine's ball in February, you certainly can manage something far more spectacular in May when there is at least a chance of decent weather, and you have Everley House at your disposal. Now, I came in to ask you to come and take the air with me. It is too fine a day not to go for a drive—it smells of spring outside and flowers and sunshine. Besides, I have a surprise waiting. Leave sorting out a guest list to Dudley. He's very good at that sort of thing, and it gives him occupation, and you have to give Dudley something to do for otherwise he is out on the street selling..." Everley paused and looked up, his mouth curved in the smallest smile. "Dudley, what small item might you sell if not gainfully employed by me?"

"Apples, your grace? My father keeps a few orchards."

With a wave of his free hand, Everley looked at Davinia again. "Ah, there you have it. Apples. You cannot wish that upon the man. You may also approve his work when he's got it done, and then I shan't have to worry over his flirting with you."

Unable to resist either the tug of his hand or the coaxing in his voice, Davinia allowed Everley to help her rise and then shook out her skirts. "I shall have to change if we are to take the air."

"No, no, first there is my surprise." He tugged her with him, heading for the front hall. He waved at the porter to open the doors and then pulled Davinia with him.

She gave a laugh. "Everley, what on...oh my!" She stopped on the stone of the front steps, one hand going to her chest, the other still caught in Everley's warm grip. Tightening her hand on his, she turned to him. "Is that—?"

"Gertie? Yes, indeed. I bought her from your brother, and that is Mab in harness with her. Took me ages to find a cob to match in size and color and to have the carriage made. It's a curricle but hung low, and you've two tigers to ride behind you so you may set a new fashion."

"Or be thought extrav...oh, heavens, are those the post boys from Old Tom's?"

The lads holding the pair harnessed to the low-hung curricle doffed their caps. She thought they looked rather fine in Everley's livery of dark blue coats, white buckskin breeches, and black boots. The ginger lad kept a grave face, but the other who held Gertie's bridle gave her a wide grin, his teeth flashing white against his dark skin. Gertie nudged him with her nose, nuzzling for a treat that he produced from a pocket in the tail of his coat.

Davinia glanced up at Everley, her skin tingling from a glow that seemed to start inside her chest. She gripped Everley's hand tighter and put her other hand on his arm. "But it's not my birthday, so what is the occasion for a gift?"

"You are. I've been remiss in a bride gift for you, my darling. I ought to have produced one after our wedding night, but I rather thought, now that the dowager has given up the family jewels for your use, you might prefer this to yet another heavy weight to hang about your neck."

With a grin, Davinia turned, stretched up and swung her arm around Everley's neck. "It's perfect. Oh, they're prefect. No...you're perfect."

Everley glanced behind him and then looked back at her. He tucked a stray curl behind her ear. "Not a bit of it...and we're about to shock the servants."

"Yes, let's do," Davinia said.

He swept an arm around her, fit his mouth to her, and kissed her until her knees had gone weak and he'd stolen most of her breath. Pulling back, but leaving his arm about her waist, he asked, "About that drive...?"

"Oh, yes, let's do. I may even allow you to take the reins from me. But only for a short time. I hope

Gertie gets along with Mab. I've a dashing new habit I've been longing to wear. Wait for me, will you?"

He gave her a firm squeeze, and a smile crooked the corner of his mouth. "For you, Davinia—forever."

Author's Notes

The Battle of Trafalgar in 1805 confirmed Britain's naval supremacy over France, but other battles continued at sea. The HMS *Monarch* saw action in September of 1806 when a French squadron with five frigates and two corvettes was intercepted by six British ships. Under the command of Commodore Sir Samuel Hood, the British gave chase. Outrun and outclassed, the French fought hard, inflicting damage on the leading British ships and wounding Commodore Hood. Eventually, the French surrendered, but this seemed a possible battle in which Davinia might have lost her sailor husband.

In the winter of 1808 and the month of February, there were reports of bad northwesterly storms affecting the east of England. Even worse winters would hit in 1811, when the Thames froze. Overall, the 1800s saw some really rough weather, but for this story we have a full moon, which, in the age of horses and no streetlights in the country, was vital to travel. The full moon fell on February 12 in 1808, and while technically the moon is only full for an instant, it appears bright for about three days before and after that moment, so it would provide for good travel on Valentine's.

As to Valentine's Day celebrations and the custom of giving cards, the holiday traces back to Ancient Rome and just kept on through the ages. The custom of giving cards came about in the 1700s, with most cards being handmade. A few pre-printed cards appear in the late 1700s. The oldest surviving example in the UK dates from 1797, when Catherine Mossday sent a card to a Mr. Brown of London. It is decorated with flowers and images of Cupid, with a verse printed around the border reading: *Since on this ever Happy day, All Nature's full of Love and Play. Yet harmless still if my design, 'Tis but to be your Valentine.*

ABOUT THE AUTHOR

Shannon Donnelly's writing has won numerous awards, including a nomination for Romance Writer's of America's RITA award, the Grand Prize in the "Minute Maid Sensational Romance Writer" contest, judged by Nora Roberts, and others. Her writing has repeatedly earned 4½ Star Top Pick reviews from *Romantic Times* magazine, as well as praise from *Booklist* and other reviewers, who note: "…simply superb…wonderfully uplifting…beautifully written…"

In addition to her Regency romances, she is the author of the Mackenzie Solomon, Demon/Warders Urban Fantasy series, *Burn Baby Burn* and *Riding in on a Burning Tire*, and the SF/Paranormal, *Edge Walkers*. Her work has been on the top seller list of Amazon.com and includes the Historical romances, *The Cardros Ruby* and *Paths of Desire*. Her Regency, Lady Chance, is a BRAG Gold Medal winner.

Reader reviews are always appreciated! For more information, visit shannondonnelly.com

OTHER BOOKS TO LOOK FOR...

Under the Kissing Bough
Will Christmas bring Eleanor Glover more than a marriage? Will mistletoe bring Lord Staines more than a wife?
RWA RITA Finalist, Best Regency Romance

A Compromising Situation
She's a governess...with a secret in her past. He is a lord, far above her station. Duty keeps them apart...But in the moonlit ruins of Rothe House...romance blossoms.
Golden Heart Winner, Best Regency Romance

A Dangerous Compromise
Clarissa is out to find a rake to reform—for she is certain that is the only path to true love. But when the rake who catches her eye is really a gentleman masquerading as such, it's going to be a battle to find out whose heart breaks first.
Finalist: Award of Excellence, Holt Medallion, Laurel Wreath

A Much Compromised Lady
What happens when the path of England's most notorious rake crosses that of a willful gypsy who wants to become a respectable lady...It can only lead to true love...Or to murder.
"...well-done and very witty... a wonderful hero, who will out-duke any duke you've ever read about." – The Word on Romance
Romantic Times Top Pick: 4½ Stars and Gold Medal

Proper Conduct
Can a proper but impoverished lady find happiness with a half-Gypsy lord who is only trying to make amends for past wrongs to her family?
Winner Winter Rose, Best Historical

A Proper Mistress
She's not really a proper mistress—it's only an act. But it's no pretense when the man who hired her to be his fiancée starts to fall in love with her.
Romantic Times Top Pick - 4½ Stars

Barely Proper
The "Wild Winslow" boys have been trouble for as long as Sylvain Harwood can remember—but when the elder son must clear his name of murder, she's ready to do anything to help. Anything except betray the love she's kept hidden from the man.
"The third of Donnelly's 'Proper' regencies is simply superb, with subtly nuanced characters and a cleverly constructed plot that is bound to please readers who enjoy expertly written traditional regencies." *John Charles - American Library Association*

Lady Scandal
4½ STARS TOP PICK – "Excitement and passion are fierce companions and the danger never ends... sure to captivate readers." -- Romantic Times Bookclub
Romantic Times Bookclub Nominated "Best Regency"

Lady Chance
Paris in 1814 is a place for intrigue and plots, but is it a place where Diana might find a lasting love with the French soldier she has never forgotten?
Bragg Gold Medallion Winner

Paths of Desire
The last thing either wants is to fall in love, but when desire leads to a passion that won't be denied, how can the heart do anything but follow?

The Cardros Ruby
During a killing Yorkshire winter frost, a country house part becomes host to hidden truths that must come out and a life that might be forfeit.

REGENCY NOVELLAS

Cat's Cradle
A lonely proper widow…and a rakish gambler who has won the neighboring manor house—can they find happiness together?

Silver Links
A lord and lady's perfect marriage...gone perfectly wrong, but can all be made right on Valentine's?

Border Bride
A run-away bride headed for Gretna Green but with one too many men traveling with her.

Stolen Away
A lord who proposed to the wrong lady all because of tangled lies and even more tangled hearts.

Davinia's Duke
A too-perfect duke, a very imperfect lady...is it the perfect match or a perfect disaster?

Made in the
USA
Lexington, KY